Over the Wall

OVER THE WALL
First published 2010
by Little Island
an imprint of New Island
2 Brookside
Dundrum Road
Dublin 14

www.littleisland.ie

First published in 2000 as *Die Welt Steht Kopf* in Stuttgart, Germany by Thienemann Verlag

ISBN 978-1-84840-944-6

Cover illustration © Annie West 2009.
Inside illustrations by Karoline Kehr.
Book design by Inka Hagen.

Printed in Ireland by ColourBooks.

Little Island received financial assistance from
The Arts Council (An Chomhairle Ealaíon), Dublin, Ireland.

The publisher acknowledges the financial assistance of Ireland Literature Exchange (translation
fund), Dublin, Ireland.
www.irelandliterature.com
info@irelandliterature.com

10 9 8 7 6 5 4 3 2 1

Over the Wall

RENATE AHRENS

Translated by

SIOBHÁN PARKINSON

Little Island

About the author

Renate Ahrens was born in Germany in 1955. After some years working as a teacher, she moved to Dublin in 1986 with her husband and has since worked as a freelance author. As well as children's and adult novels, she has written stage and radio plays and scripts for children's television programmes.

First, a few small things you need to know ...

This story is set in Hamburg, in northern Germany, in 1990, shortly after the fall of the Berlin Wall. (That's important for the story, but you can find out about it for yourself.)

Hamburg is on the River Elbe and its small tributary, the Alster. There are also many Alster canals. But when people in Hamburg speak about *the Alster* they mean the two lakes right in the heart of the city: the Inner Alster and the Outer Alster.

In Hamburg, as in most European cities, many families live in flats in apartment buildings rather than in separate houses.

Children in Germany usually change from primary to secondary school at the age of ten. School starts every day at eight o'clock. At the time this story takes place, lessons used to finish at lunchtime. (Nowadays they go on into the afternoon, like in Ireland.)

Oh, yes, and the name Rike is pronounced Reeka. The other names are more or less the same as they would be pronounced in English.

And that's enough info: now for the story ...

THERE MUST BE SOME MISTAKE

Karo lay on the grass by the swimming pool and looked at the sky. Not a single cloud. And it was warm, like summer. At her birthday party, just two weeks ago, they'd all been wearing jumpers.

Karo felt for her chain. It was smooth and cool to the touch. The best birthday present she'd ever got. It was made of silver and from it hung a pendant with a pale blue stone. Mum had been almost more excited than she was when she'd been opening it.

'The chain ... it came from your father.'

'Really?'

'He gave it to me for my twentieth birthday.'

'Why don't you wear it?'

'I ... thought, now you're eleven, maybe you'd like to wear it.'

'Such a lovely stone!'

'Come on, I'll put it round your neck.'

Mum never talked about Karo's father. All Karo

1

knew was that he'd been killed in an accident before she was born. Mum didn't even have a photo of him. They hadn't known each other very long.

Karo ran out into the hall and looked at herself in the mirror.

'Do I look like him?'

'You have his eyes, light brown and that green circle around the pupils.'

Karo went closer to the mirror. So that's where she'd got those weird eyes.

'Did you love him?'

'Yes.'

'But why don't you wear the chain, then?'

For a moment, Mum looked as if she was going to cry. She bent down to pick up the wrapping paper, murmuring that she'd better get the breakfast. Karo knew that there was no point in asking any more questions. But the good thing was – for the first time in her life, she had some kind of keepsake of this unknown father.

Karo turned over onto her tummy and fingered the light blue stone. She hadn't told anyone that the chain had come from her father.

'Hello, Karo!'

Karo looked up and saw Rike coming towards her.

'Ah, there you are!'

'I couldn't get away any earlier,' said Rike, spreading out her towel. 'All hell broke loose at home again.'

Karo grinned. All hell was always breaking loose at the Wiecherts' house.

'In the first place, my father freaked out because Alex got an E again in maths and is probably going to have to repeat the year. Then the housekeeper managed to let the broccoli soufflé burn and we had to have a takeaway for lunch, sausages and chips. And just when we'd finally eaten and I wanted to get away, my mother went through the roof because she couldn't find her car keys. Today of all days, when some big shot wants to come and see the gallery.'

'So, did you find them?'

'They were in the ignition.'

The pair of them snorted with laughter.

Karo loved Rike's stories about her chaotic family, and she loved going to the Wiecherts' because there was always something going on there. It was very quiet at Karo's.

'I wish it was like that in my house,' Rike had said recently. 'No annoying brother. No strict father. And a young mother.'

Rike thought it was terrible that her mother was getting on for fifty.

Karo could do without a strict father and an old mother, but she'd like to have had a brother, preferably an older one like Alex. He was thirteen.

'So is your brother going to have grinds?'

'He's been having them for ages. In maths and English. Four times a week.'

'Four times a week? He must be stressed out!'

'You could say that. We're dead lucky to be good at school, you and I. When I look at Alex sweating over his homework, and my mother always breathing down his neck ... '

'That reminds me. When is our next English test?'

'Friday. But it'll be no bother to us.'

Karo nodded and lay on her back again. Still not a sign of a cloud. As far as she was concerned, it could stay like this for the whole summer.

'Karo ... '

'Yeah?'

'Will we go and get our hair cut?'

Karo sat up quickly. 'Are you cracked?'

'My mother is always giving out about my blond rats' tails.'

'Let her give out,' said Karo, twisting her long dark hair around her finger. 'I like your hair.'

'Yours is much nicer, much thicker.'

'Rubbish!' said Karo and gave Rike a thump. 'Come on, let's swim!'

They swam a few races, practised their dives and swam under water until they were out of breath. Then they collapsed, exhausted, on to their towels and let the sun dry them off.

On the way home, Karo cycled by the supermarket to pick up a salami pizza for supper. She'd promised her mother, who had a meeting at school and wouldn't be home before six.

As Karo turned into the Kuhnsweg, she wondered if she should take her bike down to the basement, or would she and her mother go for a spin later, around the Alster? She decided to chain her bicycle outside on the street.

Frau Becker was in the entrance hall, with her dwarf Doberman. 'Out and about again?' She was always poking her nose in.

'Yeah. Why?'

'The children of today never seem to have any homework to do.'

'The children of today have already done their homework,' said Karo. 'Can I get past you?'

She ran all the way up to the third floor, without stopping.

'I'm just home,' called her mother, as Karo opened the door.

'How was the meeting?'

'Awful. This principal drives me mad. It's never about the pupils. It's always about official rules and regulations.'

'Will we go for a spin on the bikes later?'

'Good idea.'

'Ok, then. I'll stick the pizza in the oven.'

'Fine. And I'll give Grandpa a quick ring.'

'Give him my love. Tell him I'll drop round at the weekend.'

The pizza was nearly ready when the doorbell rang.

'Hello?' said Karo into the intercom.

No reply. Old Herr Zeuner had probably left the front door open again. Sure enough, the next time it was the bell at the apartment door that rang.

'Who's there?'

'My name is Klessmann. I'm looking for Jutta Delius.'

Karo opened the door and looked into the pale face of a man she'd never seen before. He was wearing a beret and was quite old. His accent sounded strange.

'I'll get her.'

Karo knocked on her mother's door. 'It's for you.'

'I'm on the phone.'

'She'll be with you in a minute,' Karo said to the man and went into the kitchen to check on the pizza.

The melted cheese was just the right shade of golden brown. She pulled the baking tray out of the oven and got two plates from the cupboard.

Then she heard a weird noise from the hall, like a suppressed screech. Karo caught her breath.

She ran out of the kitchen and saw that her mother and the man were locked in a tight embrace in the hallway. The beret had fallen on the floor. Karo's throat felt hot and constricted. Why hadn't her mother told her that she had fallen in love? Why did she let her find out like this? She stared at the man, who had hardly any hair left on his head, and noticed for the first time that his shoulders were trembling. He was crying. Why was he crying? And Mum? She was crying too. Karo broke out in a sweat. She didn't know what was going on. Most of all she wanted to pull her mother out of the arms of this man, to sit her down at the table and serve her a slice of pizza. But she was rooted to the spot. If only she could call out!

At last, her mother let the man go and turned slowly to Karo. Her eyes were puffy from crying, but they shone.

'Karo ... '

She was smiling. What was there to smile about?

'Karo, this is Martin,' said Mum, holding the bald man's hand.

'Who?' asked Karo, staring at the two hands, grasping each other, as if they would never let each other go.

'I don't know how to tell you ... '

'What?' muttered Karo, turning to the wall.

'Please look at me.'

'Why?'

'Martin and I ... we ... we've known each other for a long time ... '

Karo felt as if she'd been belted in the stomach.

'Karo ... '

No, she didn't want to hear any more.

Suddenly, she felt her mother's hands on her shoulders.

'Let me go!'

'Look at me.'

Unwillingly, Karo turned around, but she didn't look at her mother. She didn't want to see those shining eyes.

'Karo, Martin is your father.'

A roaring started in Karo's ears. This couldn't be. She had no father. She saw the man as if through a veil. His face was contorted. Was that supposed to be a smile?

'It's the same for me. I've only just found out that I have a daughter.'

Karo shook her head. 'I'm not your daughter. There's been some mistake.'

She ran into her room and banged the door after her. Of course it was a mistake. How could this man be her father? Her father was dead!

CRACKS IN THE CEILING

Karo was sitting on the floor, with her knees drawn up, pressing her fists against her temples. No! No! No! a voice shouted inside her head. It wasn't true. It couldn't be true. If it was true, then her mother had been lying to her all her life.

'Karo?' She heard Mum calling from outside the door.

Please let her say it isn't true, thought Karo, watching the door handle being pressed down.

'Karo,' whispered her mother.

Karo didn't move. Mum came and sat beside her on the floor and tried to take her in her arms, but Karo stiffened.

'Say it's not true!'

'Karo ... '

'Say it, before it's too late.'

'Too late for what?'

'If it's true ... '

'It's true. Martin is your father.'

'No!' shrieked Karo and burst into tears.

'At least let me explain,' said Mum, reaching for Karo's hand.

'Don't touch me!'

'Karo ... '

'Go away!'

'Listen to me first.'

'No!'

'But why not?'

'You're a liar. My mother is a common liar.'

'Karo ... please forgive me.' Now Mum started crying too.

Well, she could cry away. Karo stood up and went to the window. Through her tears, she saw that downstairs in the courtyard Herr Zeuner's two cats were fighting again. The white one was all over the black one, trying to keep it away from its bowl. They hissed and scratched, until the black one finally retreated to a corner of the yard and sat licking its wounds.

Karo could hear her mother blowing her nose. Why couldn't she just go?

'If you only knew how it all happened back then ... '

Karo turned round. 'Tell the man to go away.'

Mum stood up and looked at Karo. 'This is not getting us anywhere.'

'So?'

'This is about our family.'

'I don't know that man.'

Mum wiped her eyes and left the room.

Karo's head felt dull and woolly. She threw herself on her bed and looked at the ceiling. It was covered with fine cracks, like veins in the plaster. She wondered what would happen if the veins burst. Would it just crumble a bit here and there, or would the whole ceiling come crashing down? Karo closed her eyes and rolled onto her side. Let it come down. She couldn't care less.

It was after half past nine before she realised she was hungry. She opened the door softly and listened. Voices came from the living room. In a flash, she was in the kitchen, cutting herself a slice of the cold salami pizza, which lay untouched on the baking tray. She had hardly got the first bite into her mouth when she heard steps in the hall.

'Karo?'

Her mother had obviously been waiting for her to come out of her room.

'We've always been able to talk about everything,' said her mother, sitting beside Karo at the table.

'Has he gone?'

'No.'

'He has to go and not come back.'

'Karo, I understand that I've disappointed you, and that you're angry with me about that. I should never have hidden the truth from you. Adults make mistakes too, you know. And I am really very, very sorry. I just didn't know what else to do.'

Karo went on stuffing her face with pizza. She suddenly remembered that her bike was still out on the street. The spin around the Alster had, of course, never materialised.

'What I don't understand, though, is why you are so angry with Martin. It's not his fault.'

'It's not his fault?' shouted Karo, jumping up. 'He comes here and ruins everything. And you say it's not his fault?' She ran out into the hallway and was just about to disappear into her room when the living-room door opened and the bald-headed man came out.

'Karoline ... '

She grabbed the door handle. No, she would not talk to him. No matter how pleadingly he looked at her.

'I'm so sorry that I've caused such a lot of trouble here.'

Karo slipped into her room and shut the door. So he was sorry. Why had he put in an appearance at all? Why couldn't he have realised the havoc he would wreak? Now it was too late.

She stood in front of the mirror and looked at her eyes, puffy from crying. Then she gasped. The chain! The chain must have come from him. That was all she needed, for him to see her wearing it. She yanked it off and threw it into a drawer.

After she had got into bed and turned off the light, she thought about Rike. Would she tell her tomorrow what had happened? No. It was all so terrible, she couldn't even tell Rike about it.

Karo twisted and turned, wondering about what was going to happen next. At some stage, she looked at her alarm clock. Twenty past two. Baldy had been sitting for hours with her mother in the living room. What would she do if he decided to move in with them? Her mother needn't think Karo was going to go along with that. She'd rather go and live with Grandpa. He wouldn't mind. She and Grandpa had always got along.

ENOUGH IS ENOUGH!

When Karo came into the kitchen the next morning, her mother was just laying the table. Two mugs, two cereal bowls, two spoons. Karo was relieved. She'd thought Baldy had stayed overnight.

'Morning, Karo,' said Mum, smiling.

'Where's your man?'

'Martin's gone to a hotel. We were talking until dawn.'

'And what time do you think I got to sleep at?'

'It'll be all right. We just need time.'

Mum's voice sounded as if she was trying to convince herself. Karo poured milk onto her muesli and started to eat it. Nothing was going to be all right, as long as Baldy was around.

'Come on, let's be friends again,' said her mother, stroking Karo's hair.

'Stoppit!' hissed Karo.

Mum looked at her, shocked.

'Send that fellow back to wherever he came from.

14

I'm not going to be friends until you do that.'

'Karo, please ...'

'No!'

What the hell did Mum think? That they could just go on as if nothing had happened? It had been a nice life, their twosome. Karo could feel tears welling up again in her eyes, when she thought of all the stuff she and Mum had done together: their picnics on the Elbe, their cycling trips to Duvenstedter Brook, rowing on the Alster canals. When it rained, they would go to the cinema or to the swimming pool or ice-skating or just to have an ice-cream. And before, when she was younger, they'd had a season ticket for Hagenbeck's Zoo. They used to go to see the elephants nearly every week. Had Mum forgotten all that? Or had it never been very important to her? Had she been secretly hoping all along that one day this Baldy would turn up? As far back as she could remember, Karo had never seen her mother with a man. Rike had asked her once if she didn't find that a bit strange. Her mother was still young, after all, and good-looking too. She must have some sort of an admirer. Karo nearly fought with Rike that time. She didn't want any old admirer putting his oar in. And now along came this Baldy and wanted to mess everything up and turn their lovely twosome into a threesome. Daddy, Mummy and child. A nice, normal family. Normal, says who? thought Karo and drank her tea down in one gulp. This so-called family was anything but normal.

'Would you like schnitzel for supper?'

'I don't care,' said Karo, standing up. 'Do what you like.' She pulled on her jacket, grabbed her bag and banged the door after her.

As she passed her bicycle on the street, she wondered for a moment if she should cycle to school today, for once. That way, she wouldn't have to talk to anyone, at least not until she got there.

No, better not. Lots of bikes had been stolen from the schoolyard lately. That was all she needed.

It was as packed as ever on the bus. Karo made her way through the crowd and found a spot to stand between two fat men. Maybe she'd be lucky and Rike wouldn't notice her when she got on at the next stop. But of course Rike found her immediately.

'Hello, Karo.'

'Hello.'

'What's up?'

'Why?'

'Dunno. You look sort of weird.'

Karo shrugged.

'Had a row with your mum?'

'Hm ...'

'There was blue murder in our house last night. All because I didn't tidy my room. My father is such a fusspot. You couldn't be doing with him.'

If you only knew what is going on in my house, thought Karo. A bit of fuss over an untidy bedroom doesn't come anywhere near it.

'Then at supper my father was on at my mother. You know she wants a dog.'

'Hm ...'

'Me and Alex too, of course. But my father, with his cleanomania, says that dogs only bring dirt into the house.'

Would Rike ever just shut up about her family?

'I mean, my father doesn't have a leg to stand on. At the end of the day, he doesn't have to do the cleaning.'

Shut up, thought Karo. Shut up or I'll burst.

'Anyway, in the end, my mother stood up from the table and said: "You'll get used to the dog, once he's here." My father was seething, but I bet anything my mother will go ahead and get a dog.'

Karo clenched her fists. One more stop. Then they would be there.

'Hey,' said Rike suddenly. 'What's happened to your chain?'

'Lost it.'

'Oh, no! Did you get into trouble about that?'

'Hm ...'

'Yesterday at the pool, you definitely had it. I'm sure about that. Maybe you lost it on the way home. You were going to the supermarket, weren't you?'

'Hm ...'

'We could drop by there this afternoon and ask if they've found it.'

'Nah.'

'But why not? It was such a lovely chain. And you were so delighted to get it.'

'I don't want to,' cried Karo. 'Don't you get it?'

'Are you all right? What are you shouting about?'

Karo pressed her lips together to stop herself from yelling. Just at that moment, the bus stopped in front of the school.

They pushed their way to the exit door and Karo was relieved that for the moment they couldn't talk.

As they got off the bus, they met David and Sven, who were in their class, and who wanted to know something about maths homework. Rike explained to them how she had solved the problem, and then they started talking about Herr Kowalski, their maths teacher, who always gave too much homework. Karo wanted to tell Rike she was sorry, but she couldn't get a word out. Why did she have to fight with Rike on a day like today?

They had German first. While Frau Bruns was struggling to discuss some short story or other with them, Karo was thinking about Baldy. He didn't only talk funny; he looked funny too. That bluey grey anorak and those old-fashioned trousers with a carefully pressed crease in them. And as for his shoes. Totally out of date.

'Karo, are you dreaming?'

Karo started. Frau Bruns was standing in front of her, looking quizzically at her.

'I don't feel well.'

'Are you sick?'

'I don't know.'

'Do you want to go home?'

Karo shook her head. No, definitely not home.

Frau Bruns frowned, as if she suspected that something was wrong. Then she turned to Jonas and asked him the question instead.

'Will we get something to drink?' asked Rike at break.

'I'm not thirsty,' muttered Karo.

'Not even for a Coke?'

Karo shook her head.

'I don't understand what's going on. Can you tell me what's wrong with you today?'

Karo shrugged her shoulders and went to the window. She just couldn't tell Rike why she was in such a bad mood. But at least she didn't seem to be too cross about this morning.

When Karo turned back from the window, Rike had disappeared. Herr Lehnert, her English teacher, was there in her place, looking at her, his face bright red.

'Did you not hear the bell?'

'Oh, yeah.'

'Well, then. Out you go! And don't let it happen again!'

Karo spent the rest of the break alone, in a corner of the yard. That had never happened before. She could see Rike in the distance, standing around with Tina and Birte. Tina was telling them something, and then they all laughed. Karo wished she could join in and laugh with them.

Just before English class, she decided she would go and report sick after all. She knew she just couldn't bear the comments of stupid Herr Lehnert today without bursting into tears.

When she got home, it was a quarter past twelve. Mum wouldn't be home until two. Her bedroom door was shut. Was Baldy sitting in there on Mum's sofa?

Karo went into the kitchen and made herself a cheese sandwich. It was really spooky not knowing if she was the only person in the flat or not.

To distract herself, she opened the paper. Some time last winter she'd begun reading the paper. Shortly after the fall of the Berlin Wall. It had been so exciting. Every day there were huge headlines. Mum had talked about nothing else for weeks. And she had collected as many newspaper cuttings as she could find about it. Every second article was still about East Germany, the German Democratic Republic as it used to be called, which was soon not going to exist any more. It had just been decided to reunite Germany this year. As she thought about the word 'reunite', something suddenly stuck in her throat. Why hadn't she thought of it before! Baldy! The way he talked, the way he dressed – he must come from the East. They were allowed over into the West now.

Is that why Mum had sat for days on end in front of the TV, looking at all the people pouring in over the border? Crazy people, hugging each other, crying with happiness. Mum had cried too. Karo hadn't thought anything of it at the time because everyone's parents and the teachers too had gone a bit loo-lah about it all. The day after the fall of the Wall, Frau Bruns had abandoned their German lesson so that she could discuss the whole thing with them.

'How many of you have ever been in East Germany?' Sven was the only one.

'We were in Dresden a few years ago. We have relatives there. It wasn't bad.'

'But I bet you didn't get any oranges,' shouted David. 'They're dead scarce in East Germany.'

'It was summer time. There aren't any oranges in the summer anyway.'

'Here you can get whatever you want all year round.'

'Only in some expensive shop.'

'So what? The question was, can we get oranges here in the summer time or not, and I'm just saying, yes, we can.'

'It's stupid to eat oranges in the summer time,' said

Karo. 'There's lots of other fruit then.'

'Do you mean you think it's right what they did over there in the East?' asked Tina.

'No, of course I don't. What rubbish!'

'They're all loony over there,' said Birte and she started to giggle.

'My relatives aren't loony,' said Sven crossly. 'My relatives are perfectly normal.'

'Did your normal relatives drive you around in their Trabant, or did you have to walk everywhere?' asked Jonas, grinning.

'We drove in my father's car.'

Karo remembered how the others had all gone on making fun of Sven and his trip to East Germany, even during break. Until Sven burst out into angry roars.

Just then, Karo heard the door of the apartment opening. She started.

'Karoline?'

Baldy! It couldn't be! How come Mum had given him a key, just like that?

Karo folded up the paper and stood up. It was just as well she'd come home early and had already eaten. No way was she going to sit with him in the kitchen and answer stupid questions: how school had been, what kind of hobbies she had, what her best friend was called.

'I could cook something for us.'

Karo turned around. There he stood in the doorway

with his beret on, smiling at her.

'I've already eaten.'

'Pity.'

He was still standing in the doorway. But at least he wasn't smiling any more.

'Could I get by?'

'Certainly.'

Karo pushed by him and made for her room.

'Jutta said you don't get home until nearly one.'

'So she was wrong.'

'Karoline?'

She stood still. Now what did he want?

'Your mother and I love each other. After all these years, we still love each other just as much as we did on the very first day.'

Why was he telling her this?

'Give us a chance.'

'A chance? What kind of a chance?'

'To get to know each other.'

'Suppose I don't want to?'

He took off his beret and stroked his bald head. 'I, I always wanted a daughter.'

'That has nothing to do with me.'

He nodded and put the beret back on.

Five minutes later, Karo heard the door being closed.

She glanced into Mum's room. On the desk there was a note: 'Dear Jutta, I'm across the road in Senza Nome. Love, Martin.'

Love, Martin. Love, Martin. This Baldy was insufferable.

'Why did Martin go to Senza Nome?' asked Mum when she got home. 'He was going to cook for us.'

'I'd already eaten.'

'Did you have a row?'

'He tried to get around me.'

'Karo, don't be so contrary. If you had seen how happy he was to hear that you are his daughter!'

'But I'm not happy that he is my father.'

'Why not?'

'I don't need a father.'

'But ...'

'Leave me alone!'

Mum left the flat shortly after that. The quick tapping of her court shoes could be heard on the stairs, fading into the distance. She must be down by now. Karo looked out of the window, and sure enough, she was running across the road and almost didn't see a motorcyclist. She obviously couldn't wait to see Baldy again.

When they came back two hours later, he had a suitcase with him. It looked as if he was planning to stay at least a month.

He took off his beret and nodded at Karo.

'We fetched Martin's suitcase,' said Mum unnecessarily, pulling Baldy into her room.

Karo looked after them uncomprehendingly for a moment, then threw herself on her bed and cried. She cried with anger and she cried about this stranger who had the cheek just to turn up here. And she cried because Mum wasn't on her side any more but on the side of the stranger. Maybe that was the worst thing of all, to have been betrayed by Mum.

She had to do something. Otherwise she would burst. Suddenly she had an idea. She had more than fifty marks in her savings box. She'd go to the hairdresser's and have her hair cut off. Very short. So short that Mum would hardly recognise her!

When the hairdresser picked up her scissors, Karo clenched her teeth. She mustn't weaken now.

Three-quarters of an hour later, she hardly recognised herself. She stood in front of a shop window and looked into the face of a thin girl with closely cropped hair. Mum would freak out. And Rike? Rike too. They'd sworn to each other a few years back that they'd never go to the hairdresser's alone.

Should she go round to her place and explain? Rike would understand. Rike had always understood her.

Karo leapt up on her bike and cycled off. On the way, she thought about what she would say to Rike. 'This creature showed up at our house yesterday ... Allegedly, he's my father.' Or maybe she shouldn't mention the father thing? She could just say that her mum had a boyfriend, who seemed to come from East Germany. 'So what?' Rike would ask. 'Is that a problem?'

No, if she was going to tell her anything she had to tell her the whole story.

When Karo turned into Körnerstrasse, she saw Rike standing in front of her house with a young golden retriever. It was too much. Karo braked and did an about turn on the spot. If there was one thing she couldn't face today, it was Rike telling stories about the new dog.

AT RIKE'S HOUSE

Mum let one short, sharp screech out of her when she saw Karo. Apart from that, she said nothing.

But Rike's eyes nearly popped out of her head the next day on the bus. 'That was so mean of you! You can't get your hair cut just like that. Just because we've had a row.'

'That's not why.'

'Well then, why?'

'I'll tell you. But first, I want to say sorry about yesterday.'

'You were completely out of order.'

'Yes, I know.'

'So what was wrong?'

'Ach ...' Karo felt her throat constricting again.

'Hey, would you look at you!' came a voice they knew. It was David. He was behind them on the bus, pointing at Karo.

'Look the other way if you don't like it,' Karo called back to him.

'Was it because of the row with your mother that you were so jumpy?' asked Rike.

'Hm ...'

'Must have been really bad. I wouldn't have believed it. She is always so nice.'

'At the moment she is unbearable.'

'Just like my father.'

The word father brought Karo out in goosebumps. She hadn't seen Baldy since yesterday at lunchtime, but only because she'd stayed in her room all the time. She hadn't spoken to Mum either.

'Will we get a Coke after the English test?' asked Rike.

'Oh, I'd totally forgotten about the test.'

'Doesn't matter. It'll be a doddle.'

But in the second period, when the test was on, it was no doddle for Karo. The longer she looked at the sheet of paper, the more the letters swam before her eyes. In their place, the image of Baldy, holding Mum's hand as if he would never let it go, kept appearing. Shortly before the bell, her head cleared a bit and she managed to fill in the blanks in that part of the test, but it was too late to do anything about the grammar questions and the irregular verbs.

'I made a complete mess of the test,' she said to Rike in the yard.

'Why? It wasn't hard.'

'I dunno ... It was as if everything was all blurry.'

'It won't be so bad.'

'It will,' said Karo, starting to cry. 'It is that bad. It's even worse than that.'

Rike put an arm around Karo's shoulder. 'Will I get you a Coke?'

Karo shook her head.

'Is it the test that you are crying about?'

'No.'

'Well, then, what are you crying about?'

'Because ... because ...' But Karo was crying so hard she couldn't get another word out.

'Do you need a hanky?'

She nodded.

'Here,' said Rike, taking one out of her pocket.

It took a while for Karo to stop crying. And if Rike hadn't been standing beside her, it would have taken even longer.

'This fellow turned up at our house a few days ago,' she said, wishing she could stop crying. 'I let him in myself. And when I came back into the hall a few minutes later, there he was, hugging my mother nearly to death. I didn't know what to think.'

'She hadn't told you she was in love?'

'Nope.'

Just at that moment the bell rang, and Karo was almost pleased about that. She couldn't talk about this business of her father here in the schoolyard.

'Maybe it's a good thing that your mother is finally in

love,' said Rike, as they went back into the classroom.

'It is not one bit good,' said Karo. 'Everything has changed at home.'

In maths, Rike passed a note to her. 'Will you come over to my place after school?' it said.

'Yes, great,' Karo replied.

'OK. I'll ring home at break and say you will eat with us.'

'Super!'

'Could you two please stop writing all these notes!' called Herr Kowalski.

Karo and Rike looked at each other and started to giggle. It was good to be friends again.

When they arrived at the Wiecherts' house, they heard loud barking.

'That's Max,' said Rike.

'The golden retriever.'

Rike looked at her in amazement. 'How on earth did you know that Max is a golden retriever?'

'Because I saw you with him yesterday evening, outside your house.'

'You were here yesterday?'

'Yeah, I came around to apologise to you and to explain what had happened. But somehow, I just couldn't do it.'

Rike gave her a little thump. 'Everything is fine now. In fact, I was going to go over to you yesterday, but then my mother came home with the dog, and it has been total chaos in our house since then.'

Rike opened the door and Max shot out. He jumped up on them and licked their hands.

'Isn't he sweet!' cried Karo and hunkered down to stroke him.

'He's only six weeks old and he piddles everywhere.'

'And what has your father got to say about him?'

'He wants us to take him back. But of course my mother and Alex and I are dead set against that.'

'Hello, you two.'

Karo turned around. Frau Wiechert was standing there, smiling, with her hand out.

'It's great that you came to see us.'

'Good afternoon,' said Karo.

'Suits you, the short hair.'

'Thank you.'

'Do you like our Max?'

'A lot!'

Just then, the housekeeper came rushing in. 'This is too much! The dog has eaten the salami!'

'Don't worry, dear Frau Bergmeier,' said Frau Wiechert.

'A beast like this was all I needed!'

'We'll just have to make sure we don't leave anything out on the table.'

Frau Bergmeier gave an angry sniff and disappeared back into the kitchen.

'Oh, no,' muttered Rike. 'Now Daddy has an ally.'

'They'll get used to him,' said Frau Wiechert and rubbed Max between the ears.

'What are we having?' asked Rike.

'Lasagne with salad.'

'Mmm, yum!' Karo suddenly noticed how hungry she was.

'Can we eat outside?' asked Rike.

Frau Wiechert nodded. 'In ten minutes. I just have to make a few quick calls.'

The Wiecherts didn't live in a flat like most people Karo knew. They had a big house on the banks of an Alster canal and it even had a landing stage.

'Do you want to let your mother know that you're here with us?' asked Rike.

'Nah.'

Karo had already decided on the way here that she wasn't going to ring Mum. She could work it out for herself that Karo preferred to eat at Rike's.

'Come on, let's go outside,' suggested Rike.

Max slithered over the polished wood floor and was at the door out onto the patio before they were.

In the garden, Alex was lying in a hammock, grinning.

'Well, you two? Is the old man here yet?'

'Haven't a clue,' said Rike. 'Did you get another E?'

'No ...'

'So what is it, then?'

'Not telling you.'

'If it's something that's going to annoy Dad, don't tell him until after we've eaten. Let's have a bit of peace today.'

'What is he not to tell me until after lunch?'

Karo shrank. Herr Wiechert was standing behind them, looking very smart in his dark blue three-piece suit. Maybe solicitors had to look like that. Herr Wiechert never wore ties, only bowties. Today it was one with blue and red stripes. Karo liked Herr Wiechert, even though Rike got so worked up about him.

'Good afternoon, Karoline.'

'Good afternoon, Herr Wiechert.'

'Well, then, Alexander, spit it out.'

While Alex was getting slowly out of the hammock, Herr Wiechert was trying to shoo Max away. But Max appeared to have a soft spot for him. He kept coming back to him and licking his hand.

'This slobbernig dog is intolerable!' shouted Herr Wiechert.

'He's perfectly tolerable!' cried Rike and Alex.

Herr Wiechert flopped onto a chair, sighing. 'Everyone is always ganging up on me.'

'Yes!' cried Rike and Alex.

Suddenly, Herr Wiechert looked serious again. 'Alexander, I'm listening.'

'But you're not to give out.'

'That depends.'

'I've been ... made captain of the hockey team.'

'Wonderful! Congratulations!' cried Herr Wiechert. 'You deserve it!'

Alex beamed.

'Good news for once,' said Rike.

Max lifted his leg and piddled in a flowerpot. Karo, Rike and Alex burst out laughing, while Herr Wiechert simply shook his head wordlessly.

They'd just sat down at the table and were about to start their meal when the phone rang.

'Oh, no!' groaned Frau Wiechert. 'That'll be for me.'

But it was Mum looking for Karo. Karo's good mood disappeared on the spot.

'Where are you?'

'I'm having lunch at Rike's.'

'Why didn't you let me know? I've been worrying.'

Karo didn't answer.

'We're having spaghetti with tomato sauce.'

'Well, enjoy!' said Karo and hung up. Did Mum think she could get around her just by cooking her favourite food?

'Everything all right at home?' asked Frau Wiechert when Karo came back to the table.

Karo nodded, but she didn't look anyone in the eye.

Later, listening to music in Rike's room, Karo wondered if she should tell her the rest of the story.

'How long has your mother known this fellow?' asked Rike suddenly.

Karo swallowed. 'For ages.'

'So why has she kept him a secret all this time?'

Karo closed her eyes. How could she put it?

'Is there a problem with him?'

'What do you mean?'

'Well, you know ... does he drink?'

'I dunno.'

'Or ... has he been in jail?'

'I don't think so.'

'Well, she must have some reason, mustn't she?'

'He looks as if he comes from East Germany.'

'Really?'

'The way he dresses. And he talks funny.'

'But how did your mother meet someone from East Germany?'

'Haven't a clue.'

'Was she in Berlin, maybe, when the Wall came down? All these people were hugging each other, people who'd never clapped eyes on each other before.'

'Nah, that was only six months ago. My mother has known this fellow much longer than that.' Karo stood up and went to the window. 'She studied for a while in Berlin.'

'That's ages ago.'

'About twelve years.'

'Before you were even born.'

Karo stared out into the garden. Max was barging about among the flowers.

'My mother claims this fellow ... is ... that he's my father.'

'Whaaaat? I thought your father was dead.'

Karo turned around to face Rike. 'I thought that too. Until the day before yesterday.'

'And until then, there wasn't a squeak out of him, because he wasn't able to get out of East Germany?'

'I suppose ...'

'Did you not ask your mum?'

'No. She keeps trying to tell me stuff, but I don't want to know.'

'But why not?'

'Because I don't want a father!' cried Karo, and she could feel another crying fit coming on. She shrank back and put her hands over her face. How come nobody could understand how she felt?

'Don't cry,' said Rike, putting her arms around her friend. 'Is that why you cut your hair?'

Karo nodded. 'That fellow ... I wish he would just go away, and never come back.'

'But if he doesn't?'

'They might just get a surprise.'

Karo suddenly remembered the chain. Every time she touched her neck, she noticed that something was missing.

'Bloody chain,' she muttered.

'Why?' asked Rike. 'What has the chain got to do with anything?'

'It came from him,' replied Karo, blowing her nose. 'That's why I don't wear it any more. He gave it to my mother as a present, in the old days.'

The two girls sat in silence for a while.

'Would you like to stay here for the weekend?' asked Rike.

Karo looked at Rike and nodded. 'If your parents don't mind.'

'They won't. I'll phone Mum at the gallery and check with her.'

When Rike came back, she was beaming. 'All well. But she said you should ring home first.'

'Did you tell your mother what is wrong?'

'Yes. Was I not supposed to?'

'No, that's fine.'

Mum answered immediately. When Karo told her that she wanted to stay at Rike's for the weekend, there was silence at the other end of the line.

'And ... then what?'

'If that fellow hasn't gone by Sunday evening, then I'll move in with Grandpa.'

'Aha. I still can't understand why you got your hair cut. Without a word to me.'

'And I made a total mess of my English test today. That never happened before either.'

'Ach, Karo, that's not so bad.'

'It's bad!' shouted Karo, hanging up with a clatter.

She was sure her mother would ring back immediately, but nothing happened.

'So, what did she say?' asked Rike as Karo came back into the room.

'Well, she wasn't exactly over the moon, but she didn't say no.'

'Will we go for a row?'

Karo nodded. She was lucky to have Rike. Otherwise, she would go stark, staring mad.

ONE NIL TO KARO

It was a warm, sunny weekend. Karo and Rike rowed on the Alster canals, they went swimming and played for hours with Max. They had such fun that Karo sometimes forgot all about Baldy.

They were sitting on the patio having iced chocolate on Sunday when the phone rang.

'Good afternoon, Frau Delius,' they heard Herr Wiechert saying.

Karo's heart beat harder. Was Mum ringing to say that Baldy had gone and she could come home?

But Mum didn't want to speak to her; she wanted to speak to Frau Wiechert. What was that all about? Not good, thought Karo.

It took for ever before Frau Wiechert came back to the patio. She looked serious.

'Karo, your mother is in a state. She wants you to come home at once.'

Karo stared at her iced chocolate. She didn't feel like having any more of it.

'I thought Karo could stay until this evening,' said Rike.

'Yes, but now her father has decided to go back to Berlin tonight if Karo won't see him.'

Karo pricked up her ears. She'd almost done it!

'He blames himself because Karo has been so upset at his appearing out of nowhere.'

And well he might, thought Karo.

'The whole situation is very difficult for all of you,' said Frau Wiechert, putting a hand on Karo's arm. 'But it's no good putting your head in the sand.'

Karo gulped.

'Your mother wants you all to sit down quietly and discuss the whole thing.'

'The three of them?' asked Rike.

'Yes. It's all about Karo and her parents.'

Karo jumped up and ran into the house.

'Look, don't run away like that!' Frau Wiechert called after her.

Karo locked herself into the bathroom and pressed her forehead against the cold tiles. Parents. Parents. How she hated that word!

Loud voices could be heard coming from the patio.

'You can't just send Karo back!' Rike sounded indignant.

'But her mother is insisting.'

'She doesn't want to go home.'

'Rike, I can't do anything about that.'

'Oh, you're so mean!'

Rike was the only one who was really on her side, thought Karo, opening the door. She got her bag from Rike's room and was just about to sneak off when Max came at her like a shot.

'Bye, Max,' murmured Karo.

Suddenly, Frau Wiechert was there too. She stroked Karo's head.

'Karo, you can come back any time if your mother lets you.'

'Thanks.'

Rike came with her to the garden gate. 'I'll keep my fingers crossed for you.'

'Why?'

'That it won't be so bad.'

'Maybe I won't go home at all.'

'So where would you go?'

'I dunno ...'

'Look, give it a try at least.'

Karo shrugged her shoulders. 'We'll see.'

'See you tomorrow.'

Karo went slowly along Körnerstrasse and then turned into Mühlenkamp. What was she going to do now? Every bone in her body objected to the idea of sitting down at home with Mum and Baldy for a chat. What was there to discuss? The whole thing was perfectly clear. Baldy had to go. And apparently he'd already twigged that it would be for the best if he went back to Berlin today.

Karo stood still and wiped her forehead. Why did she have to do this? She'd much rather go swimming. She'd have to go home for her swimsuit, though – she'd borrowed one over the weekend, but she'd left that behind. And of course Mum wouldn't let her go again. If only she had her bicycle! Then she could go cycling around until Baldy had left. Or she could visit Grandpa. Yes, that was a better idea. She had the key to the basement where the bikes were kept. She'd try to sneak into the basement and get her bike. If there was nobody out on the balcony, and Mum wasn't bringing down the rubbish to the bin just at that very moment, then it should all go smoothly.

Kuhnsweg was totally still in the dead heat. Karo squinted up to the third floor. As luck would have it, the balcony was empty. And there wasn't a sinner in the basement either.

A few minutes later, she was cycling in the direction of Eimsbüttel.

'What a surprise!' cried Grandpa, taking her bag. 'And you've got a new hairstyle too.'

'I thought I'd pay you a little visit.'

'Would you like hot chocolate or would you prefer orange juice?'

'Orange juice.'

'Luckily, I just happen to have a couple of cream-cheese croissants.'

'Oh, yum!'

When they were sitting in the kitchen munching their croissants, Karo started to tell Grandpa about Baldy.

'I can't stand the fellow.'

Grandpa sighed. 'It's certainly a tricky situation.'

'Does Mum really think I'm just going to swallow this whole?'

'No ...'

'I don't want a father!'

'She's very worried about you, Karo. But on the other hand, she is so happy.'

'Was she not happy before?'

'Oh, yes. But this man is the love of her life. She says he's a wonderful person.'

'Sounds like something out of a soppy love story,' snapped Karo.

'The kind of person who keeps his cool, when she's going up the wall.'

'All I know is that he has ruined everything.'

The phone rang.

'I bet that's Mum,' said Karo.

'Did you not tell her you were coming here?'

'No.'

Grandpa picked up the receiver. All Karo could hear was him muttering. Then he hung up.

'She's pretty damn angry, but you can drink up your juice.'

When Karo got home an hour later, Frau Becker met her in the entrance hall on the ground floor with her quailing dwarf Doberman.

'You've got a visitor, haven't you?'

'Not me.'

Frau Becker looked around to see if anyone was listening, and then she whispered into Karo's ear: 'So what's the story with that man who's been going in and out of your place these past few days?'

Karo hesitated. Then she had a brainwave. 'That's my mother's new amour.'

'Her new ... what?'

Karo giggled. 'Amour. Don't you know what an amour is?'

Frau Becker frowned.

'A lover.'

'Really?' Frau Becker stared at her with her mouth open. 'And I always thought your mother was such a respectable person.'

'A mistake easily made.'

Karo climbed the stairs slowly. A lover wouldn't be

a problem. In comparison with this fellow, who claimed to be her father.

Mum was sitting in the living room reading. Baldy was nowhere to be seen.

'Why did you go to Grandpa's instead of coming straight home?'

'I just wanted to see Grandpa.'

'You knew perfectly well that Martin and I wanted to talk to you.'

'Exactly.'

Mum sighed.

'I thought you were bloody stupid, ringing up the Wiecherts like that.'

'I'm sure you did.'

Karo threw her bag into the corner. 'Has he gone?'

Mum slammed her book closed and stood up.

'Well, tell me.'

She sighed again. 'Martin left half an hour ago.'

'At last!' cried Karo.

'Back to Berlin.'

'To East Berlin?'

'Yes,' said Mum, looking at her in surprise. 'How did you work that out?'

Karo grinned. 'You can tell he's from the East.'

'Don't be so snooty.'

'Who else goes around looking like that?'

'You haven't the first clue what you are talking about.'

'All I know is that fellow is an embarrassment, going around in that weird gear.'

'Is it so important, what he wears?'

'Not any more. Now he's gone.'

Mum shook her head. 'This is not the Karo I know.'

'And I hope he never comes back!' cried Karo, flopping down onto the sofa.

'He was so happy to be here with us.'

'I've had a great idea,' said Karo and she started to giggle.

'Aha?'

'It'll solve all our problems.'

'So, out with it!'

'East Germany just builds the Wall again.'

Mum stared at her, aghast. Then she disappeared into the kitchen.

Karo stretched out on the sofa and started whistling. One nil to her. Mum could think what she liked of her. The main thing was Baldy had got the message – there was no room for him in their lives.

THE CALM BEFORE THE STORM

'So, how did it go?' Rike asked on the bus on Monday morning.

'He's gone.'

'Then you did go home after all?'

'Yeah, but first I went to see my grandfather.'

'And what did your mum say to that?'

'She was pretty cross. Still is.'

'So what are you going to do now?'

'Nothing. She'll get over it.'

And so she did. Mum was quieter than usual, but Karo just let on not to notice. And within a few days, things were back to normal.

When Karo came home on Friday with a D minus in her English test, Mum put her arms around her and said something about a once-off and that she shouldn't worry about it. She never mentioned Baldy any more. It began to feel to Karo almost as if the whole thing had just been a bad dream.

'Would you like to go to the movies tonight?' her mother asked at breakfast.

Karo nodded. 'We haven't done that for ages.'

'That's right. *Cinema Paradiso* is on in the Abaton.'

'Is that the one about the little boy who loves going to the cinema?'

'Yes, that's it.'

It was all just the way it used to be. They cycled along the Alster. It was all people eating ice-cream or taking their dogs for a walk. At Kleine Rabenstrasse they turned right towards the university, where Mum had been a student. Every time they went past the student canteen, Mum would show Karo the green bench where she had sat one time when she felt sick. It was the day of her English exam, and she only barely made it into the exam hall. It was before Karo had started at school. She used to go to a playgroup; she remembered it well. She was always the last one to be picked up, because Mum had so much studying to do for her exams, as well as teaching in a language school.

They cycled past the bench today, but Mum never said a word. Karo was just about to call out to her that she'd forgotten her spiel about the bench, but then she didn't. Mum had evidently decided that it was a silly game, this thing about the bench. Or maybe she just didn't think of it. Maybe she was thinking about Baldy. No, that was rubbish. Baldy was long gone, and he hadn't written or rung up either. She'd noticed that.

In the foyer, they bought a bag of popcorn and two packets of mints. Mum met a colleague of hers from school, but she shook her off pretty quickly. It was going to be just the two of them, she whispered in Karo's ear. Karo thought that was a bit over the top. It was no skin off her nose if Mum's colleague wanted to sit with them.

Their favourite seats, in the middle of the third row from the back, were free. Karo had just flopped into her seat and started to eat her popcorn when she stopped short. A few rows in front of them sat a man who looked just like Baldy.

'What's up?' asked her mother.

At that moment the man turned around and waved at someone. He was at least twenty years younger than Baldy.

'Nothing,' said Karo. 'I just thought I'd seen some-one you know.'

The film absorbed Karo so completely that she forgot everything around her. The way that little boy struggled to get to go to the movies – it was so funny and at the same time so sad. And the way the film projectionist who kept chasing him away at the start got to be friends with him at the end, even though he was much older – old enough to be his father. The bit where the little boy rescued the man from a fire, but couldn't save him from blindness, made Karo cry. And Mum cried too. Karo cuddled up, and her mother put an arm around her and held her tight. They hadn't sat like that since before Baldy showed up. Karo closed her eyes for a moment. How good Mum smelled! She'd almost forgotten.

That evening, Karo began to think that maybe she and her mother were a twosome again. And nobody was going to be able to break up this twosome any more.

'Have you heard from – um – your father at all?' asked Rike two weeks later. They were eating ice-cream at the swimming pool.

'Nah. He's gone. And he's staying gone.'

'Do you really think so?'

'For sure. Why, what do you think?'

'I don't know. He could always come back to Hamburg some time.'

'Ah, rubbish! And you can drop the father.'

'How come? I mean, he is your father, isn't he?'

'Yes, well, maybe he is my biological father, but that

doesn't make him a real father, not by a long shot.'

'So what do you call him?'

Karo grinned. 'Baldy.'

'Is he totally bald?'

'Not totally. He has a few wisps of hair, I suppose.'

'So he's pretty old?'

'Ancient.'

'And what does your mother say about him being gone?'

'Nothing.'

'Nothing at all?'

'No.'

'Weird.'

'What do you mean?'

'She was so happy when he turned up.'

'Well, maybe she's happy now that she has a bit of peace.'

Rike looked doubtful.

'There's no need to look like that! Everything's fine at home these days.'

'That's good,' said Rike, but she didn't sound so sure.

'Come on, let's get in the water!' shouted Karo and she jumped up. She'd had enough of this conversation about Baldy.

But on her way home, Rike's question wouldn't go away. Suppose she was right to be so doubtful? What if Baldy really did come back to Hamburg some time? No – he wouldn't dare! And even if he did, Mum would send him on his way. Mum was on her side now. She knew that.

BOMBSHELL

When Karo came home from school a couple of days later, there was a letter for her mother in the mailbox. From Berlin. And the sender's name was given as M. Klessmann. Karo swallowed. What was Baldy doing writing to Mum now all of a sudden? Or could it be that this wasn't the first letter? Had Mum just not told her about the others? It was usually Karo who brought the post up from the mailbox. But not always. Had Mum been trying lately to beat her to it? Could it be that Mum and Baldy were hatching something?

Karo ran upstairs, the letter burning her fingers. Should she read it? She could easily steam open the envelope and stick it back later. Or should she just throw it away? No. It would come out some time if she did that. She decided to put the letter on Mum's desk and to say nothing for the moment.

Mum carried on all afternoon as if nothing had happened. It wasn't until that evening, when Karo was already in bed, that she mentioned the letter.

'You saw I had a letter from Martin today.'

Karo said nothing. She just looked up at the ceiling.

'It seems to us, things have calmed down a bit in the last few weeks.'

Karo began to count the little cracks in the plaster.

'And we thought, maybe we could give it another go.'

Three, four, five, counted Karo.

'Martin has been thinking of us all the time since he left Hamburg.'

Six, seven, eight.

'And I've been thinking about him too, of course.'

Nine, ten, eleven.

'Sometimes I've wondered if you've been thinking about him also.'

That ceiling was going to come down some day soon.

'Maybe you're not ready to talk about it yet.'

Karo didn't move.

'Have a good sleep, then, and we'll talk about it in the morning.'

Mum stroked her hair and kissed her on the forehead.

Karo still didn't move. And she said nothing either. From now on, she wouldn't say a single word at home. Not even if her mother stood on her head.

It wasn't long before Karo got used to saying nothing. She even started to enjoy it. Her mother kept trying to get her to talk. Sometimes she asked her to be sensible. Sometimes she begged her not to make everything worse. Sometimes she shouted at her to stop acting the clown. But Karo stuck to her guns, even over the week-end. As long as she kept mum, Baldy wouldn't come. She was sure of that.

'Has your father come back?' asked Rike on the bus on Monday.

'What makes you ask?'

'I saw your mother with a man yesterday.'

'Where?'

'On the Alster.'

'You can't have!'

'The man was half bald and he was dressed very differently from people around here. He was definitely from the East.'

Had Baldy been in Hamburg for ages, living in some hotel somewhere?

'I thought he looked nice.'

Karo's head started to whirl. If she didn't get off this bus, she was going to be sick. She pushed past Rike, making for the door.

'Hey, Karo!' Rike called after her. 'Where are you off to?'

Luckily, the bus stopped just then. Karo got out

and ran off, without turning back.

It was twenty to eight. They had maths first. If she ran, she could just make it to school on time. And if she didn't run, Herr Kowalski would give her a late mark.

Karo spotted a bench. If she sat here in the sun, instead, Herr Kowalski would think she was sick. Rike might let it slip that she'd seen Karo on the bus, but that wasn't very likely. And even if she did, Karo didn't care.

She sat down and stared at her feet. She hadn't said a word to Mum for six days. What did she have to do to make her see how annoyed she was with her? Mum had cheated on her in the meanest possible way. For weeks, she'd carried on as if everything had gone back to normal. And Karo had fallen for it. She hadn't had the foggiest idea that Mum and Baldy were in cahoots. And then, when she'd found the letter and the cat was out of the bag, she had been sure Mum was going to tell Baldy to go to hell. But instead, she'd let him come to Hamburg and she'd been meeting him on the sly. It was all too much!

Quarter past eight. Should she go to school for the second lesson? It was German. No. She'd rather take the underground somewhere. Maybe she'd go into town. She'd never been in the city centre on her own before.

On the journey, she had this weird feeling that a stranger was going to speak to her at any moment, asking what she was doing, sitting here in the underground, instead of being at school. But nothing like that happened. And as she climbed up the steps at Jungfernstieg, she laughed at herself for even thinking such a thing.

It struck her as odd that the shops were still closed at that hour. It was easily a quarter to nine. She strolled around the side streets, took a look in the windows of Hennes & Mauritz, and at half past nine she was the first person into the music department of the Alsterhaus department store. She listened to a couple of CDs, and then she wandered off to the clothes section. She tried on all sorts of jeans and millions of T-shirts, before she went looking for gym shoes. From the sports department, she went to the shoe department, and then back into the sports. In the end, she found exactly the right pair of Nikes. The only problem was that she had no money, apart from one mark thirty-five, which she exchanged for a scoop of chocolate ice-cream and a nutty bar.

By now it was twenty past eleven. If she didn't want Mum to know she'd been skiving off school, she couldn't go home until half past one. She'd never have thought she'd find it so hard to put in a morning in the city centre. She was going down Poststrasse for the third time, when, just for a change, instead of going on to the Gänsemarkt, she turned into the Grosse Bleichen.

She nearly missed the sign saying Central Library. Was a central library the same as any other library? She hadn't got her library card with her, but maybe they'd let her in anyway.

The library was on the fourth floor. Karo had just pressed the button for the lift when an old lady came toddling over.

'I always like it when I have company in the lift,' said the woman with a smile.

Karo smiled back and let the old lady go ahead of her.

'What school do you go to?'

'Lerchenfeld Gymnasium.' Karo's voice sounded hoarse. She hoped the woman wasn't going to ask what she was doing in the city centre at half past eleven in the morning.

'I used to teach German and history until a couple of years ago.'

A retired teacher – that was all she needed! Any minute now this one would say it straight out, that Karo was mitching.

'I think it's great the way children visit the library these days,' said the woman as they arrived on the fourth floor. 'Are you doing a project or what?'

Karo paused. A project – the very thing!

'That's right,' she said.

'What on?'

'The Berlin Wall,' replied Karo, without giving it a second thought.

'How interesting! Well, I hope you find lots of information.'

The woman waved goodbye and disappeared off into the newspaper section.

Karo looked around to see if anyone wanted to check her library card, but the librarians were busy with other things. She strolled along the shelves till she got to the children's section. One of the first books she opened was about a girl whose parents were getting divorced. Karo sat down and began to read. Funny how the feelings that the girl in the book had were not much different from the ones she'd had herself since Baldy had turned up. In both cases, it was all about a family that was destroyed. It seems it doesn't make much difference whether a father comes or a father goes.

When she looked at her watch, it was just after one. She'd got through nearly half of the book. Maybe she'd come back tomorrow to finish it, she thought on the way down. She could tell Rike this afternoon that she was in bed with a temperature and ask her to let Frau Bruns know.

When she got home, Mum asked how school had been. Karo went into her room without a word and closed the door.

'I'm not putting up with this for much longer!' she heard Mum calling.

Well, you're just going to have to, thought Karo, throwing herself onto her bed.

'Were you running a temperature this morning on the bus?' asked Rike when Karo called her that afternoon.

'Eh – yeah,' said Karo. 'I suddenly felt very hot, and my head started to spin.'

'And what am I supposed to say to Bruns?'

'That I have the flu.'

'Oh, right. Tina has it too.'

'Aha ...' That was good. In that case, Frau Bruns wouldn't ask any questions.

'Would you like me to call round tomorrow?'

Karo bit her lip. 'I think I'm contagious.'

'That's a pity.'

As she hung up, she felt guilty about lying to Rike. But there was no other way to get a few days off.

The following morning, she waited in a doorway until her mother drove off. Then she caught a number 108, which went straight to the central station. From there she took the underground to Jungfernstieg. She had brought a book with her because the central library didn't open until ten, and she had to fill in the time until then. Luckily, it wasn't raining, and she was able to sit on a bench by the Inner Alster.

At ten o'clock on the dot, she entered the library. This time, a librarian came straight up to her and asked if she could be of assistance. Karo told her about her project and followed the librarian to the politics section. After she'd flicked through a coffee-table book about East Germany, she high-tailed it to the children's section to find the book about the girl with the parents who were getting divorced. Every time the librarian showed her face, Karo pretended to be taking notes. Every now and again she asked a question, which wasn't very difficult. There'd been loads of discussion about the Berlin Wall at school.

In the afternoon, Karo lay on her bed, bored. The sun was shining, and she'd love to have gone to the pool. But she couldn't risk it, because she'd be sure to meet someone from school.

The doorbell rang. Karo sat up like a shot. Could that be Baldy? She would go ballistic if it was.

'Hello, Rike,' she heard her mother saying.

Rike? Karo held her breath, hoping Rike wouldn't mention anything about the flu to Mum.

The next minute, the door opened and Rike came in.

'Hi, Karo.'

'Hello.'

'Would you like an apple juice with sparkling water?' asked Mum.

'Please,' said Rike.

Karo said nothing. Mum looked at her questioningly, but Karo looked away.

Even so, Mum brought two glasses and a bowl of a certain kind of vanilla biscuits that Karo was very partial to.

'Do I sense a bit of an atmosphere between you two?' asked Rike, as Mum closed the door after her.

'Well, put it this way: I'm not talking to her.'

'Why not?'

'Because she's a cheat. For weeks, she was making up to me, taking me to the cinema, going on as if everything was the same as before, And then ... then I find out, totally by chance, that ... she and Baldy had been writing to each other all along.' Karo started to cry.

'Hey, Karo,' said Rike, putting an arm around her. 'Don't cry.'

'And then yesterday you said you'd seen them together by the Alster.'

'Is that why you skipped school?'

Karo nodded.

'I thought so. You sounded weird on the phone yesterday.'

Karo dried her tears. 'I'm sorry I lied to you. I just couldn't bear it in school any longer.'

'What do you do all morning?'

'I go to the central library and read.'

'Where's that?'

'In Grosse Bleichen.'

'In the city centre?'

'Mmm ...'

'Have you been there before on your own?'

'No.'

'Come back to school,' Rike begged. 'It's so boring when you're not there!'

Karo gulped.

'Then at least we can go swimming in the afternoons. Or you can come around to my place and we can play with Max.'

'If I stop mitching now, then it's all been for nothing.'

'I don't understand.'

'I want to make serious trouble, drop a bombshell, and I want my Mum to be so upset that she sends Baldy away for good!'

'And when is this trouble supposed to break out?'

'Dunno. It could take a while.'

They were silent for a bit, and then Rike stood up.

'Will I come again tomorrow?'

'Yeah. And you won't tell anyone?'

'Of course I won't.'

Trouble broke out sooner than Karo expected. The very next morning, as it happened. She'd just arrived in the central library, and had taken a new book off the shelf, when she saw Baldy at the other end of the aisle. He looked at her as if he couldn't believe his eyes. Karo threw the book on the table, ran to get her bag out of the locker and took the lift down. She was seething with rage. There could be only one explanation: he'd been spying on her. This bald bloke from the East was nothing but a nasty little sneak, who'd been following her about so that he could catch her out at the first possible opportunity. Karo clenched her fists. It was so unfair. Other people had normal fathers from Hamburg or Munich or Cologne. David's father was French. That was OK too. Why did Mum have to fall for this bald fellow from the East, of all people?

She roamed around the city for hours, wondering where she should go next. A few times, she tried to call Grandpa, but he wasn't there. She wanted to go away. A long way away. And not for a few days, but for good. Preferably to boarding school. Only, boarding schools were expensive. There was no way Mum could afford it. Well, Baldy was just going to have to cough up. She thought it had said in the paper recently that there were rich people in East Germany too. Of course, those were people who were loyal to the government. But why shouldn't Baldy be one of those? Anyway, it was only right that he should have to pay something for her. If he really was her father. He had eleven years to make up for, after all.

At the central station, it occurred to Karo that she could just get on a train and go off someplace. To Rome or Paris or even Bad Reichenhall, where Mum's older sister, Aunt Elke, lived. But after she'd watched the trains coming and going for a while, she lost her nerve. And anyway, she was hungry.

When she got home, Mum was in the kitchen reading the paper. No sign of Baldy.

'Hello,' muttered Karo and winced, because she'd broken her silence without meaning to.

'I think it's time you and I had a serious conversation,' said her mother, folding the paper over.

'You sound like a teacher.'

'I don't give a hoot what I sound like. Martin tells me he saw you this morning in the central library.'

'Couldn't wait to spill the beans, could he? That's to be expected, I suppose. Is he in your room?'

Mum shook her head. 'How long have you been mitching?'

'So you're interrogating me now, are you?'

'Karoline, I'm the one asking the questions. I want you to answer me – and I want you to do it now!'

Karo pursed her lips. Her mother had never spoken to her like this before.

'When did you start skiving off school?'

Mum's nose twitched. Karo stared at the tiny blond hairs that grew in her nostrils. Since when had Mum had nose-hairs? Karo grinned, thinking that the whole situation was what you might call pretty hairy.

'This is not a laughing matter.'

'Maybe it is.'

'Karoline, I'm warning you. My patience is running out. If you don't tell me right now how long it has been since you have been to school, you will see a whole new side of me.'

'Don't shout at me.'

'I will shout as much as I like.'

'If you shout at me, I won't say another word,' said Karo softly. 'And you know how long I can keep that up for.'

Mum gave one short snort and then disappeared into the living room. Karo got a bag of crisps out of the cupboard and started to stuff her face with them. She wasn't going to let Mum get anything out of her.

A moment later, she heard her mother ringing someone. She tiptoed out into the hall and listened. It was about the school work she had missed in the last few days. Was it Frau Wiechert that she was talking to? Then she heard the name Bruns. Karo blenched. Had Mum dared to phone Frau Bruns to snitch on her?

She yanked the living-room door open just in time to see her mother hanging up.

'Who were you talking to?'

'Your class teacher.'

'Have you any idea how mean you are?'

'No, but now I know that you've been missing since Monday.'

'It's not fair to tell tales. You've always told me that.'

'I wasn't telling tales. I just needed to find out how long it was since you had been to school.'

'As far as I am concerned, that's telling tales.'

'Frau Bruns thought you had the flu.'

'Yes, and it would have been much easier if you'd let her go on thinking that.'

'I am not prepared to play games like this. I warned you earlier, but you are really going too far, Karo.'

Karo ran into her room and banged the door. But Mum came in after her anyway.

'I want to be on my own.'

'And I want to talk to you.'

Karo turned her back and stared out of the window. Neither old Herr Zeuner nor his cats were anywhere to be seen down in the yard.

'Martin wants what is best for you.'

'Did you send him to spy on me, or was that his own idea?'

'Nobody was spying on you. Martin often works in the library. He caught sight of you by chance.'

'By chance? Don't make me laugh.'

'Karo, that is a ridiculous idea. We would never spy on you.'

'Do you not think it's strange that you haven't asked me one single time why I have been skiving off from school?'

'It isn't hard to guess.'

'Really?'

'You are unhappy, and I am at the end of my tether.'

'I am not only unhappy. I am furious!' screamed Karo. 'First, you let on you have nothing to do with that fellow, and then you let him come here and you meet him on the sly.'

'On the sly? We didn't meet on the sly.'

'You never said a word to me about it. I heard about it from Rike.'

'You weren't talking to me. How could I discuss anything with you?'

'So now it's my fault? That you are living a double life! Am I crazy or what?'

'A double life! What rubbish!'

'It's not rubbish! It's the truth!'

'Ach, Karo ...'

'Don't "Ach, Karo" me!'

Mum sighed. 'Frau Bruns and I have agreed to meet tomorrow, to discuss the whole situation.'

'So does that mean you are going to tell her all about your man?'

'Yes.'

'No!'

'I will tell her that this is a difficult time for you, because you have to come to terms with the idea that, all of a sudden, you have a father.'

'I'm warning you!'

'Karo, there is no point in going on as if Martin didn't exist. Everyone is going to find out about him eventually. Your schoolmates, your teachers, the neighbours. There are rumours going around already.'

While her mother was talking, Karo thought about Frau Becker, who was sure to have spread the story about Frau Delius's lover like wildfire. Well, people could gossip all they liked about Mum. Serve her right.

'Are you listening to a word I have been saying?'

'Huh?'

'I've just been saying that maybe we should go together to see Frau Bruns.'

'No way!'

'But I thought you got on well with her.'

'I don't want to talk to Bruns about it, and I don't want you to talk to her about it either. Get it?'

Karo could have sworn she heard someone coming into the flat.

'That's Martin,' said her mother.

'Who else?'

'Jutta?'

It sounded as if he was right outside Karo's door. Karo's hackles rose. No way was she going to let him into her room.

'I'm coming,' Mum called back.

'Go to him,' said Karo. 'I have nothing more to say to you.'

'Let's have lunch together.'

'No, thank you.'

'Please, Karo.'

'Do you imagine I would want to sit down at the table with people who snitch on me?'

'Have it your own way,' said Mum, as she left the room.

Karo had had it up to here. In no time, she had packed her pyjamas, some clean underwear and her swimsuit. She took her schoolbag and opened the door softly.

She could hear Martin's voice in the living room. And Mum sobbing. Cry away, thought Karo. Much good it will do at this stage.

She crept across the hall and then she was on the stairs. Hopefully Grandpa had got home by now. If not, she'd just have to wait for him. And then she would explain everything to him. If she knew Grandpa, there was no way he would send her home.

'Of course you can stay,' said Grandpa, when she arrived at his door. 'But do you not think this is going to make everything worse?'

'It can't get any worse,' Karo replied, and she told him the whole story.

An hour later, Mum rang and asked to speak to Karo, but Karo shook her head.

'She doesn't want to speak to you,' Grandpa said into the mouthpiece.

Mum seemed to yell something down the line that

Karo couldn't make out, but Grandpa got suddenly very red in the face.

'Don't yell at me! You want to know why I am taking her side? Because I don't think you can force Karo into this new family life of yours.' Then he hung up.

'Thank you,' said Karo.

Grandpa looked whacked. 'Are you hungry?'

'Starving.'

Grandpa heated up a pot of thick pea soup. Karo didn't like pea soup, but she kept that to herself. Otherwise, Grandpa would only start on about how everyone starved during the war and how thrilled they'd have been to have a bowl of pea soup.

'Your mother won't give up so easily,' said Grandpa, as they sat to the table.

'Me neither,' said Karo. 'Let's just wait and see who holds out longer.'

AT GRANDPA'S

'Hello, Karo!' called Rike in astonishment as Karo came into class on Thursday morning.

'Remember that bombshell?' said Karo softly, unpacking her bag. 'Well, it fell yesterday.'

'Is that why you weren't home?' whispered Rike.

'How d'you mean?'

'I tried to visit you at about three.'

'Oh, I forgot!'

'Your mother looked as if she'd been crying.'

'Hm ... We had a terrible row! I'm living with my grandpa now.'

'It must have been absolutely awful.'

Karo nodded and just managed to tell Rike what had happened before Frau Bruns came in. She told Karo to find out about the work she'd missed. She never said a word about the telephone conversation she'd had with Karo's mother.

'I saw you yesterday at lunchtime,' called Jonas at break.

'You can't have.'

'I did. At the central station.'

'I was in bed all day yesterday.'

'I'm sure it was you.'

'Maybe Karo has a double,' cried Sven.

Karo didn't hear what Jonas said to that. She was watching, stunned, as Mum got into her blue Golf on the other side of the street. So, she had been to see Frau Bruns. Karo wouldn't have believed it.

'What's wrong?' asked Rike.

'I've just seen my mother. She is so mean. She went to see Bruns, even though I told her not to!'

'Because you've been mitching?'

'Nah, to tell her about Baldy.'

Karo was so annoyed, she'd like to have gone off on the mitch again. But Rike managed to persuade her to stick it out until the end of school and then to go swimming with her in the afternoon.

Just as Karo got back from the pool, the phone rang.

'Your mother,' said Grandpa and handed Karo the receiver.

'Would you not reconsider?' Mum's voice sounded as if she'd been crying again.

'Why did you go to see Bruns?'

'Karo, I told you yesterday that I had to talk to Frau Bruns about the new situation.'

'And I told you I didn't want you to do that.'

'Karo ...'

'But you just went behind my back and you've been telling her things that have absolutely nothing to do with her.'

'I didn't go behind your back. You knew all about it. And maybe you will be pleased to know that Frau Bruns was very sympathetic.'

'I'm not interested in that.'

'Karo, come home.'

'No. I want to go to boarding school.'

'That's nonsense!'

'It's not. That fellow will have to pay for it.'

'Just listen to me: there is no question of boarding school. And you can't stay with Grandpa either.'

'Why not?'

'Because it is too much for him.'

'He says I can stay.'

Mum sighed. 'Where did you sleep last night?'

'On the sofa in the living room.'

'And how did you get to school?'

'On the underground.'

'Which train?'

'The U2. It goes from Osterstrasse direct to Mundsburg.'

'But you must have to get up earlier.'

'I know.'

There was a silence, in which Karo wondered if she

should ask Mum if she'd bring her some clothes over and a few things for school. Otherwise she'd have to go back home, which she really didn't want to do. Mum would try everything to keep her there.

'Could you please tell me how long you plan to stay with Grandpa?'

'Until that fellow has left,' answered Karo.

More silence at the other end of the line. Karo picked up a pen and began to write a list of the things she'd forgotten yesterday, in the rush: her toothbrush, her Walkman, her gym shoes ...

'I suppose you think I'm going to bring things over for you?'

'No, but ...'

'What do you need?'

As she read the list out to Mum, she had a lump in her throat. She had a sudden rush of homesickness for her own room, her bed and the view from her window.

'And what about your bike?'

'I have that here.'

'But there's no basement for bikes at Grandpa's.'

'I know. Last night, I chained it to the fence.'

'If it's nicked, I'm not buying you another one.'

'Don't threaten me! Do you really think that I'd come home because we have a bike basement?'

It was Grandpa who took in the suitcase. From the kitchen, Karo could hear Mum telling him what a business he had got himself mixed up in. Having an eleven-year-old around was no picnic. And he knew perfectly well that he was supposed to take things easy. Grandpa muttered something that Karo couldn't quite catch. As she left, Mum extracted a promise from him to let her know if Karo's visit was too much for him.

It wasn't the first time that Karo had slept over at Grandpa's. A few years ago, when Mum had had to have her appendix out, Karo'd stayed with Grandpa for ten days, and at that time she'd been amazed at his funny little ways.

When he was reading a book, he always kept a thick cushion on his stomach. Because that was more comfortable. He was right. Karo had tried it.

On top of that, Grandpa never watched television. He just listened to the radio. News, plays, educational programmes and especially programmes in foreign languages. 'You're the lucky child,' he used to say. 'I wish I could learn a new language at my age.'

The one thing Karo couldn't get used to was the smell of onions. Every morning Grandpa ate two pieces of crispbread with cream cheese and onion rings. He didn't keep the cut-open onion under the glass food bell that Mum had given him expressly for this purpose, but put it on a saucer in the cupboard where he kept the crockery. Mum swore every time she opened the cupboard and the stink of onions hit her. But Grandpa wouldn't hear of doing it differently. 'In my own flat, I can do what I like, and anyway, I like the smell of onions.'

That evening, Karo fell asleep, thinking that she would be staying for some time with Grandpa; at least until the summer holidays, and maybe even longer than that.

Mum called every day to find out how Karo had got on at school, and whether she'd had tests or got the results back, and to remind her to help Grandpa in the kitchen.

'You don't have to keep telling me to help him. I know that myself.'

'And what about your laundry?'

'What about it? Grandpa and I have just come back from the laundrette.'

'And are you eating properly?'

'Today we had meatballs with caper sauce.'

'You don't like those.'

'I like the ones Grandpa makes.'

'Even the capers?'

'Yes, why not?'

Mum harrumphed, as if she didn't believe Karo. 'If you like, I could call over later. We haven't seen each other for a week.'

'I'm seeing Rike this afternoon.'

'Then maybe I'll come this evening. I could bring you your bicycle pump.'

'I picked that up the day before yesterday.'

'And you didn't come upstairs?'

'Nope ...'

She heard Mum gulping.

'Well then ... I'll be seeing you.'

Karo wanted to tell her how weird it had felt, coming into the entrance hall and slipping down into the basement. But Mum had already hung up.

Frau Bruns seemed to sense that Karo didn't want to talk to her about what Mum called 'the whole situation'. Once or twice, at the end of a German class, she had looked over at her inquiringly, but Karo always looked quickly away.

But then, she appeared beside her in the schoolyard one day and said she could just imagine how Karo was feeling, and she wanted her to know that she could come and talk to her at any time. Karo nodded and ran off quickly, because she didn't want Frau Bruns to see her tears.

'Frau Bruns asked me something today,' said Rike, a few days later.

They were lying on the grass beside the swimming pool, looking at the sky.

'What?'

'She wanted to know if I knew if there was any way we could help you.'

'Well, there isn't.'

'Are you going to stay with your grandpa for ever?'

'Dunno.'

Rike turned onto her tummy and looked at Karo. 'I asked my parents if you could come and live with us. We have loads of space.'

'And? What did they say?'

'They don't think that would work. It wouldn't be fair to your mum.'

'Pity. I'd love to move in with you.'

'Me too. It'd be great,' said Rike, rolling onto her back again.

Karo closed her eyes and imagined what it would be like to live at the Wiecherts' house. Rike's father was pretty strict at times, but he could also be very funny. And Rike's mother was hardly ever strict. Alex was a good laugh, even if he got up Rike's nose sometimes. And Max of course was super.

'Karo?'

Karo jumped.

'Would you mind if I got my hair cut too?'

Karo sat up. 'No, of course not.'

'I've been thinking about it for a few days. You look so fab with your hair short.'

'It would suit you too.'

'D'you think?'

'For sure.'

'Will you come with me?'

'What? Now?'

'Yeah. Otherwise I'll lose my nerve.'

'Have you got enough money with you?'

'I brought some specially.'

Later, as they were celebrating Rike's new hairstyle in the ice-cream parlour, Karo spotted Mum and Baldy crossing the street. They were arm in arm, laughing. Karo gulped.

'What?' asked Rike.

'My mother ... she was just there, with that fellow.'

'Where?'

Karo pointed across the road. 'Over there.'

'Ah, yes. That's the man I saw her with on the Alster that time.'

'Let's see where they are going,' suggested Karo.

'OK, then.'

While Rike was paying, Karo didn't let the pair out of her sight. Now they were turning left into Mühlenkamp.

'It looks as if they are going home to your house,' said Rike.

'Could be,' muttered Karo, pulling Rike after her.

Just before they reached Mühlenkamp Karo slowed down. Maybe Mum and Baldy were window-shopping at the bookshop, just around the corner. Who was to know?

'You go on ahead,' she said to Rike.

Rike disappeared and then she came right back. 'They've gone.'

'Funny. They were there just two minutes ago,' said Karo, looking around her.

'Why are we following them anyway? I thought you didn't want to have anything to do with them.'

'I just wanted to know what they do when they are together.'

'They'll be in one of the shops. If we just mosey along, we'll find them easily enough.'

'Nah, it's stupid. They'll see us for sure.'

Rike stopped up short and indicated with her thumb towards the flower shop. 'They have already.'

Then Karo saw them too. Baldy was carrying a big pot with a Paris daisy in it, and Mum had a bunch of yellow roses in her hand. She waved at them. Baldy didn't have a hand free, or he'd definitely have waved too.

'Come on,' said Karo. 'Let's go.'

She turned on her heel and ran back to the ice-cream parlour, where they'd left their bikes chained up.

'Weird,' said Rike, as they pedalled along the Alster a little while later. 'First you go looking for that pair, and then you run away.'

'So what?'

'So you're not as indifferent to them as you pretend.'

'I am!' shouted Karo. But she knew that Rike knew that that wasn't true.

'Since when has Rike had short hair?' asked Mum when she rang that evening.

'Since today. We went to our hairdresser in Poelchaukamp.'

'So that's how come we saw you.'

'Hm ...'

Neither of them said anything for a moment. Then Karo started to tell her mother about school. She didn't want Mum getting the idea that she'd been spying on her and Baldy.

SO WHAT WAS IT LIKE IN THE OLD DAYS?

'Would you like to come to lunch again?' asked Rike a few days later. 'Or would your grandpa not allow you?'

'Oh, no, he lets me do nearly everything.'

'Actually, my parents and I want to ask you something.'

'What?'

'Wait and see.'

The next day, Karo went home with Rike after school. They had hardly opened the door when Max came racing at them, licking their hands off.

'I do believe he's grown again,' said Karo.

Frau Wiechert nodded. 'Considering how much he eats ...'

'Good afternoon, Karoline,' said Herr Wiechert, putting out his hand.

'Hey, Karo,' cried Alex. 'Have you heard? I'm going to be allowed to move up a year after all.'

'That's great!'

'Yes, Alexander's been lucky again,' said Herr Wiechert. 'And all because he has his English teacher wrapped around his little finger.'

'No way! It was all my own hard work that did it.'

'You and hard work? That'd make a fine change.'

'Right, this discussion is at an end,' cried Frau Wiechert. 'It's time to eat.'

'What are we having?' asked Alex.

'Goulash with beans and mashed potatoes.'

'Can old Bergmeier not cook something decent for a change?' muttered Alex.

'If that doesn't suit you, you can cook your own meals in future,' said Herr Wiechert. 'Really, that boy!'

'Herbert, please ...' Frau Wiechert sighed.

'Spoilt or what?'

'Oh, come on, let's just eat,' cried Rike.

It looked like rain, so they sat indoors today, at the big dining table that Rike's parents had inherited. It could seat at least twelve.

Herr Wiechert had calmed down and didn't even complain when Max lay down on his feet.

'That dog ...'

'Max loves you,' said Rike.

'As you know, I never wanted a dog.'

'And now you couldn't live without your foot-warmer,' laughed Alex.

'Oh, well,' said Herr Wiechert with a smirk. 'I suppose I would miss him.'

'That's why we are going to take him with us on our summer holidays,' said Frau Wiechert.

'And while we're on the subject ...' said Herr Wiechert.

'Exactly,' cried Rike.

Karo didn't know what on earth was going on.

'We have taken a house in the south of France for three weeks,' said Rike. 'And we were just wondering if you'd like to come with us.'

'Do you mean it?'

'Yes.'

'We're off on Friday week. Straight after school.'

'I don't know if my mum would let me.'

Frau Wiechert smiled. Had she been talking to Mum already, on the quiet?

'The best thing would be if you gave her a ring after lunch.'

As Karo ran to the phone, she suddenly realised how excited she was. She'd been trying not to think about the summer holidays lately, because she was dreading them so much. Sitting silently with Mum on a deckchair at the seaside, on the Baltic. Or silently climbing some mountain or other in the Alps with Mum. That was what they had done in the last few years. And they'd enjoyed it so much! This year they would enjoy nothing to-gether. She would far, far rather go on holidays with the Wiecherts. There was always something going on with them, but that wasn't the only reason. She liked the Wiecherts, and the Wiecherts liked her. When she was in their house, they made almost no difference between her and Rike. Karo liked that. Sometimes, she caught herself wishing she was really their daughter. Then she'd have a proper family, with a father and a mother, a brother and a sister ... and a dog.

'Delius,' answered Mum.

'It's Karo.'

'Hello, Karo. Where are you?'

'At Rike's. The Wiecherts have invited me to go to the south of France with them. For the first three weeks of the holidays. Can I?'

Mum sighed. 'Frau Wiechert rang me yesterday.'

'And?'

'I'd hoped that ...'

'What?'

'That we could have a holiday together.'

Who did she mean by 'together'? Was she including Baldy in that?

'Do you want to go?'

'For sure!'

'It's an awfully long way.'

'I know.'

'And you don't speak the language.'

'The Wiecherts are sure to be able to speak French. They go to France a lot.'

'But are you sure they don't mind having you along?'

'No problem. Otherwise, they wouldn't have asked me. Max is coming too, by the way.'

'Who is Max?'

'The Wiecherts' new dog.'

Mum sighed again.

'Please!'

'Oh, all right. It's fine by me.'

'Really?'

'Yes.'

'Thank you!'

Karo was just about to hang up when she realised that Mum had something more to say.

'Karo?'

'Yes?'

'I thought I'd come round tomorrow afternoon to you and Grandpa.'

'Why?'

'Because I miss you.' Mum's voice sounded suddenly sad. 'We haven't seen each other for three weeks.'

'Hm ...'

'I'll bring some cake.'

'Fine.'

Karo hung up and went back slowly to the others. She missed Mum too. In spite of everything that had happened.

The Wiecherts were delighted to hear that Mum was going to let her go. They showed her a photograph album with pictures of the house, which they'd had last year too.

'It's only five minutes to the beach,' said Rike.

'The place is called Soulac and it's not far from Bordeaux,' said Herr Wiechert.

'Were you ever at the Atlantic before?' asked Alex.

Karo shook her head.

'There are enormous waves. Fantastic for surfing, I can tell you.'

At that time in ten days, they would be in the car, ready to go. Karo could hardly believe it.

Mum could hardly believe it either, or so it seemed. The next day, she came to Grandpa's with a strawberry gateau.

'This Soulac place is so far away. And you are only eleven.'

'Eleven is pretty big,' said Karo.

'So it is,' said Grandpa.

'You two always stick together,' cried Mum, laughing, as she started to slice the cake.

Grandpa winked at Karo, and Karo winked back. Yes, she could depend on Grandpa.

They talked about school, about Grandpa's health and about the bad weather. The only thing they didn't talk about was Baldy.

After an hour, Mum got up to go. She put her arms around Karo and gave her a hug.

'When will you come to do your packing?' she asked.

'The day before we go.'

Karo saw how disappointed Mum was. She'd probably hoped that Karo would move back home before the holidays. But as long as Baldy was there, Karo woudn't even consider it. And he was sure to be there still.

'Have you met ... that fellow?' she asked Grandpa at supper.

'Martin, you mean?'

Karo nodded.

'Yes, a few times.'

'Where?'

'I went to tea once at your house. And one Sunday, we had breakfast together. That weekend when you were at Rike's. Oh, and then we went for a walk once by the Elbe, and afterwards we had a fish supper.'

'I didn't know you'd done all that.'

'Have you got a problem with that?'

'No, but I thought ... well, I thought you didn't want to have anything to do with that fellow either.'

'Why not?'

'Because ...' Karo's eyes filled with sudden tears.

'Because you don't want anything to do with him?'

'Mmm ...'

'But Karo, I was curious. I wanted to meet your father.'

That word. That awful word.

'And I have to say, I like him.'

And on top of that ... why couldn't Grandpa just say he thought he was a right thick and as boring as hell?

'I know you don't like to hear me saying this ...'

'Absolutely!'

'But there you go. That's how it is.'

For a while, neither of them spoke.

'So, did you believe Mum back then?' Karo asked at last.

'When?'

'When she told you and Grandma that she was pregnant and that the father had been killed in an accident.'

'I believed her, but Grandma didn't.'

'Why not?'

'She thought it was all a bit odd, the way she didn't even have as much as a photo of your father, and he didn't seem to have a family who wanted to see the child. I tried to explain to her that Jutta had only known him for a short time. And you don't get to know the family just straight off like that. But that didn't make the slightest impression on Grandma.'

'So she had her suspicions?'

'Well, she thought that some man had dumped your

mother. And of course she thought that was terrible. How could such a thing happen to us? She kept moaning about it.'

'Did she not help Mum?'

'No.' Grandpa took his glasses off and rubbed his forehead. 'No, she didn't help her one little bit. She was ashamed.'

Suddenly Karo understood why Mum hardly ever talked about Grandma. And when she did, why it put her in such a bad mood.

'But this ... this Martin. He did dump her, didn't he?'

Grandpa looked at her in surprise. 'No, he didn't.'

'So what did he do?'

'Well, you know how it was, that business of the border. In those days, an East–West romance didn't stand a chance. And anyway, Martin was married.'

'Well, then!'

'No, it's not what you think,' said Grandpa, and his voice was suddenly serious. 'It was your mother who left Martin, because she thought his wife was more important to him. But his marriage was already long over. The only thing that tied him to the family was his son.'

'He has a son?'

'Yes. He was five at the time.'

That meant she had a half-brother!

'Shortly after your mother left Berlin for good,

Martin applied for a divorce. He never got over the break-up with your mother.'

'He could have written.'

'And so he did. But the only address that he had for your mother was her Berlin address, and she'd already left that place. All his letters came back.'

If the son was five at the time, then he must be sixteen or seventeen now.

'Are you still listening?'

'Yeah.'

'Martin is a fine person. You'll find that out for yourself one day.'

Grandpa's words stung Karo. Later, as she was drifting off to sleep, she tried to forget what she had heard. But Martin's image kept popping up before her eyes. He was standing at the border, not able to get across.

HOLIDAYS AT LAST!

A week later, it finally started to get warm again. Just in time for the holidays.

'If only we didn't have to get these stupid reports tomorrow!' moaned Sven.

Karo didn't care about reports. All she thought about was going home afterwards, to pack.

'Cross your fingers for me.'

'What for?' asked Rike.

'That this ... Martin fellow isn't there.'

'Well, even if he is. You're only staying one night.'

Martin wasn't there, but there were a few shirts and a pair of trousers in Mum's room that must belong to him. And on the wall, beside her desk, there was a big photo of him. He was wearing his beret and smiling.

When Mum went shopping later, Karo took another look at the photo of Martin. There was something about him that she hadn't noticed before, something she'd rather wasn't there. Something kind, something warm. Karo went right up to the picture to see what kind of eyes he had. Yes, they were light brown and the pupils had a green ring around them. The same eyes as she had.

'Martin is spending the night with a colleague of mine,' said Mum, when she came back from the shops. 'You won't have to meet him.'

'Thank you,' murmured Karo.

'It was his idea.'

'I see.'

'He didn't want to spoil our evening.'

For a moment, neither of them spoke.

'Have you packed your identity card?'

'Yes.'

'And the French money?'

'That too.'

There was spaghetti with tomato sauce for supper and afterwards fromage frais with strawberries. But Karo had no appetite.

'Do you not like it?'

'I don't know ...'

'Travel nerves?'

'Hm ...'

'Promise me you won't make any trouble for the Wiecherts.'

'What do you mean, trouble?'

'Well, Rike and you, sometimes you can be a bit much. And don't swim out too far or wander away from the grown-ups, and do what Rike's parents tell you.'

'Well, of course.'

'That's fine, so.'

'Where are you going on your holidays?' asked Karo after a while.

'I'm going to Berlin for a few days. And then Martin and I are planning to go to Boltenhagen for a couple of weeks.'

'Where's that?'

'On the Baltic. In Mecklenburg.'

'Does he go there often?'

'Yes, he used to go there as a child.'

Karo looked at her plate. He'd probably gone there often with his son, then. Her half-brother. She wondered if Mum had already met this half-brother.

'Karo, if you'd like to come with us ...'

'No.'

'That's fine.' Mum stood up and started to clear the table. 'I just wanted to let you know.'

'Have you got the address of the house in Soulac?'

'Of course I have.'

'So maybe you could drop me a line?'

'For sure.' Mum suddenly had tears in her eyes.

When she was saying good night, Karo almost whispered in her ear that she was looking forward to seeing her again. But was that really true? Would it not all go back to the way it had been before, after the holidays? Fighting and leaving home. Maybe she would end up in a boarding school after all.

The next day, Karo forgot all about how it would be after the holidays. First there were reports, and then – off to France!

Rike and she got all A's and B's. Karo even got a B again in English, in spite of that D minus that she'd got in one of the tests.

Mum picked them up from school and drove them direct to the Wiecherts' house.

When Karo hugged her goodbye, she had a lump in her throat. Why couldn't Mum just come along?

'I've written it all down, where you can contact me, if there's a problem of any sort,' said Mum, giving her a piece of paper with Martin's address and the address of the guesthouse in Boltenhagen.

'Thanks.'

'Mind yourself!'

'Yes.'

Mum said goodbye to the Wiecherts, then she got into her car, gave a little wave and off she went.

Karo folded the piece of paper and stuck it in the side pocket of her rucksack. She didn't know if she would write to Mum or not, but there was no way she wanted to lose this piece of paper.

A quarter of an hour later, she was sitting in the Wiecherts' Volvo, which was packed to bursting point, and they were on their way to Elbbrücken.

'I hope the roofrack will hold up,' said Herr Wiechert, mopping his brow.

'I screwed it down really tightly,' protested Alex.

'I'm only saying.'

'Has the dog had a drink?' asked Frau Wiechert, pointing at Max, who was panting in the luggage section at the back of the car.

'I don't know,' replied Rike.

'It was your job to give him water.'

'I forgot.'

'Oh, no!' groaned Herr Wiechert. 'Does that mean we'll have to stop in Stillhorn?'

'Yes.'

All the same, they got as far as Strasbourg that day. As they drove over the French border, Karo's heart was beating hard. She'd only ever been abroad once before, in Austria. But that was different. They spoke German there.

They slept that first night in a little guesthouse, where the people already knew the Wiecherts. In the early morning, Karo woke up, bathed in sweat. Where was she? What kind of a weird bed was this? She was just about to call for her mother when she saw that Rike was sleeping next to her.

She got up quietly and went to the window. The garden was bathed in a milky light. The sun would be up soon. She could feel her eyes filling with tears. Why this sudden longing for Mum? She got the piece of paper out of her rucksack to check where Mum was now. Berlin: 9th–13th July, it said, Boltenhagen: 14th–28th July. That meant they were still in Hamburg. Should she give her a quick call before breakfast? Mum had given her change so that she could ring from a public phone. No. Karo put the slip of paper away again. Better not. Otherwise she would start crying.

She must have fallen asleep again, because when Rike shook her by the shoulder, it took forever before she was properly awake.

'It's nearly a quarter past six,' said Rike. 'We're leaving at seven. It's going to be hot today.'

And how hot it got! Max's tongue was hanging out of his mouth after two hours of driving.

'I wonder if this heat can be doing the dog any good,' asked Herr Wiechert.

'I asked you that recently,' replied Frau Wiechert. 'But you said that Max absolutely had to come.'

'Me too,' cried Rike.

'He'll survive,' muttered Alex.

They decided to get out of the car more often, to get fresh water for Max.

Karo was impatient to see how the landscape would

change. They'd been travelling south now for ages. But the meadows and fields still looked just the same as in Germany. And she hadn't seen a single palm tree yet.

But soon after they came off the motorway, she saw her first umbrella pine, and after that came a whole forest of them. It was shady and cool here. And the ground was sandy. It couldn't be much further now.

'Soon you'll see the ocean,' said Rike.

And there it was, right in front of them. Karo was amazed, as she always was, when she first saw the sea again after a long time. It was so immense. And here it was totally blue. Lucky that she hadn't rung Mum. Otherwise, she might be well back in Hamburg by now.

'We'll be there in ten minutes,' said Herr Wiechert.

Just at that moment, Max started up a horrible wailing.

'It's OK, Max,' said Rike, rubbing his head. 'He knows he's going to get out of here in a minute.'

They stopped in front of a lovely old house with a balcony and a big garden. The agent was waiting for them with the key. Rike's parents didn't understand everything she said, because she spoke so quickly. But after a while they cottoned on. A municipal water pipe had burst, and they wouldn't have any water until eight that evening. It was half past five.

'And I was looking forward so much to a shower,' moaned Herr Wiechert.

'It doesn't matter,' said Frau Wiechert. 'We can just go for a swim.'

It was high tide, and the waves thundered onto the beach.

'Be careful, children,' said Herr Wiechert. 'Waves like this are not to be trifled with.'

'They're super!' yelled Alex, throwing himself into the water with his surfboard.

Shortly after that, they saw him a long way out, riding the waves. It looked so easy.

'It's terrific, the way he can do that,' said Karo.

'Yes, Alex is a born surfer,' said Frau Wiechert with a sigh. 'All the same, I just can't look at him.'

'Come on,' cried Rike, catching Karo by the hand. 'I know a sheltered spot. The waves are not so dangerous there.'

They ran along the broad beach till they came to two breakwaters, not far apart, and between them the waves were way gentler.

Karo watched how Rike first dipped under the waves and then let herself be carried back onto the strand on the crest of a wave.

'You have to give it a go now,' she cried from the water.

The first time, Karo completely lost her footing. She was spun through the water and was eventually thrown onto the sand. She lay there for a moment, exhausted.

'You all right?' asked Rike, helping her up.

'Yeah.'

'It's not much like the Baltic, is it?'

'You can say that again.'

The second time, it all went a bit better. At some stage, Karo got the knack. Mum would be astonished if she could see her now.

'OK, you two dolphins,' called Frau Wiechert, as they came out of the water. 'Having fun?'

'Yay!'

As they were drying themselves, they noticed Max trying to run into the water. But at the last moment, he ran away from the waves. Then he jumped up on Rike with a pleading look, as if she could help him out.

'The sea is making him fidgety,' said Frau Wiechert.

'Alex is addicted to it,' said Herr Wiechert. 'He can't get enough of it.'

'Let's have dinner,' called Frau Wiechert, waving at Alex. 'If you want to eat, you'll have to come.'

Later, they sat on the veranda of a restaurant and ate grilled fish and chips. They had Coke with it and for dessert vanilla ice-cream with chocolate sauce. The air smelt sweet, the cicadas chirped and it was still so warm that they didn't need to wear their jackets.

Karo suddenly froze. A man was crossing the street in front of her, and he looked exactly like Martin. The same height, the same bald head. A boy was running along beside him. He might have been sixteen or seventeen. The boy was telling the man something, and the two of them were smiling. They came nearer and nearer. Karo held her breath. What would she do if it really was Martin? Martin with his son. Her half-brother. No! No, it wasn't he. His eyes were completely different, and anyway he spoke French.

'What's wrong?' asked Rike.

'I thought that was Martin,' replied Karo softly.

'Where?'

'That man there with the boy.'

Rike shrugged. 'He doesn't look a bit like him.'

Karo closed her eyes for a moment. What was wrong with her? Was she seeing things, or what?

The sun was shining again the next day. Rike and Karo went to the nearby supermarket to get breakfast: French sticks, butter, jam and milk. Karo wished she could understand even a little bit of this language. It sounded so lovely and at the same time so strange. One day, she would learn French, and then she could go shopping in the small shops too, and not only in the supermarket where everyone just served themselves.

They had their breakfast in the garden, under a shady tree. Then they went to the beach again.

'Put on lots of sunblock,' said Frau Wiechert. 'The sun is very strong here.'

Karo didn't burn easily, but Rike did. So from

midday onwards they lay in the shade of the two big sun-umbrellas that Herr Wiechert had set up on the beach.

'I'm so glad you came,' said Rike.

'Me too,' said Karo, looking towards the ocean.

She wondered what Mum and Martin were doing now. They were still in Hamburg today. If the weather was good, they might go picnicking to the Duvenstedter Brook or to the Elbe. She'd love to know what Mum had told Martin about her. Did he know she'd got the chain for her birthday? And how thrilled she'd been about it, because she finally had something from her father?

'Karo?'

'Yes?'

'You look so sad, all of a sudden.'

'I ... was just thinking about Martin.'

'And?'

'Really, I don't know a thing about him.'

'True.'

'Oh well, it doesn't matter. Let's go swimming!'

Karo jumped up and made for the waves. Rike followed her, and together they ducked into the first wave.

'It does matter, though,' said Rike, as she came up for air.

Karo didn't answer. She just threw herself into the next wave. Rike was right, of course. It did matter.

After a week, a letter came from Mum from Berlin. It was hot there too.

'I'm exploring East Berlin. I mean, I'm revisiting all the places that I used to go to with Martin. Everything looks nearly the same as it did twelve years ago, which seems odd to me, because so much has changed for us. In the old days, there was no you, and I can't imagine that any more. Martin neither, actually. He sends his best. We think about you a lot and wish you a really happy holiday with Rike. Lots of love, Mum.'

'What does she say?' asked Rike.

'That she's in Berlin.'

'I'd like to go there.'

'And that it's hot.'

'Is that all?'

'No. What they're doing and all ...'

Rike looked at her, frowning, but she didn't ask any more questions. Karo wouldn't have known how to answer her anyhow. But she was pleased that Mum and Martin thought about her so much.

That night, Karo dreamt that she was walking by herself on the beach. Suddenly she saw a black dot in the distance, which kept getting bigger. She was surprised, because she had never before seen anyone coming towards her here. It was a man wearing a bowtie. How weird, to go around on the beach in a bowtie. Not even Herr Wiechert did that. It was only when she was just a few metres from the man that she saw that it was Martin. He was smiling at her, but Karo pretended not to recognise him and went quickly past. But after she'd gone a few steps, she turned around towards him. He stood there, watching her. Hello, she said. Hello, Karoline, he said, and put out his hand to her. Just at that moment, she woke up.

'Is something wrong?' asked Rike.

'What do you mean?'

'You've been twisting and turning.'

'I ... was dreaming.'

'Something bad?'

'No.'

'Good.'

When Karo woke up the next morning, the first thing she thought of was the dream. If it had all really happened, would she have turned back to Martin, or would she just have kept going?

'Look, there's the bloke you pointed out to me the other day,' said Rike, when they arrived at the beach.

Now Karo saw him too, the man with the bald head. He was sitting a few metres away in a deckchair. She still thought he looked a bit like Martin.

'And there's his son,' said Rike, pointing to a boy who was just running into the water with his surfboard.

The waves were higher than usual today, and only a

few surfers could manage to stay on their boards for more than a few seconds. Alex was easily the best. Karo was astonished how fearlessly he rode the waves.

She and Rike tried a few times to duck through the waves, but the undertow was so strong that they were carried away immediately.

'Come on, let's go back onto the beach!' called Rike. 'It's too dangerous.'

'Alex should come in as well,' said Herr Wiechert.

'Alex!' called Frau Wiechert, waving.

But Alex had suddenly disappeared.

Frau Wiechert blenched. 'I just saw him a second ago.'

'Alex!' yelled Herr Wiechert.

'We need to get help!' Frau Wiechert ran up to the sea rescue people, Herr Wiechert running behind her.

Karo took Rike's hand. If only Alex was safe!

As the rescue boat was speeding out, they saw that the bald man had jumped up and was shouting something into the wind. And then it all happened very quickly. The boat braked, two lifebelts were thrown overboard and, shortly after that, the men pulled two boys into the boat. A few moments later, they were all back on the beach.

Frau Wiechert was crying when Alex got out of the boat and she put her arms around him.

'Your man there was screaming for help,' said Alex, pointing to the boy who was being helped out of the boat by the men. 'I tried to rescue him, but I couldn't get through the current.'

The bald man hugged his son and stroked his head. Karo gulped. If it had been Martin's son!

'That was bloody close, my boy,' said Herr Wiechert with a sigh.

Alex nodded. 'I couldn't have held out for much longer.'

'Why didn't they raise the red flag ages ago?' asked Frau Wiechert.

'There it is!' called Rike pointing to the flagpole, where the red flag was just being raised.

The man turned to Alex and said something in French to him. Alex looked a question at his parents.

'He's thanking you,' Frau Wiechert translated. 'Because you saved his son's life.'

'I just held out my board to him.'

'And that's probably exactly what saved him. He'd lost his strength and was just about to drown.'

'There's his board!' called Alex, pointing to a surfboard that was just being carried onto the beach by the waves.

'And where's yours?' asked Rike.

'Probably gone.'

The man said something else in French.

'He'll buy you a new surfboard,' Herr Wiechert translated.

'Really?'

The man nodded.

'Thank you,' said Alex.

The fathers swapped names and addresses and the two boys shook hands, and then they all went home.

That evening, Karo wrote to Mum. She wrote about the lovely old house, about the beach and the sea. And about how great she thought French was, and that she could already say a few words. But she didn't say anything about the boy who had nearly drowned today.

'Bye for now. Lots of love, Karo.'

And what about Martin? Should she say hello to him also? She thought for a few minutes about what she should write. 'Give my best to Martin'? Or 'Kind regards to Martin'? Neither of those sounded right. So in the end, she didn't say anything.

Karo had just got back from posting her letter to Mum the next morning when the man and his son came by. They wanted to go into town with Alex to buy him a new surfboard. Karo glanced at him secretly from the side. No, he didn't really look like Martin. His mouth and nose were quite different. And besides, he didn't have those laughter lines around the eyes.

Karo watched them going to the car. And suddenly she felt sorry that she hadn't sent best wishes to Martin in her letter to Mum.

HOME AGAIN

How could three weeks of holidays go by so quickly? Suddenly, it was the last time to do everything. The last time to buy French sticks in the supermarket. The last time to have breakfast in the garden under the tree, to swim in the waves, to walk on the beach and to hear the cicadas in the evening.

'We'll have to be off very early in the morning,' announced Herr Wiechert. 'So you'd better pack all your things today.'

'Are you looking forward to going home?' asked Rike, when they finally got to bed that night.

'I don't know.'

'So what's going to happen at your house?'

'I don't know that either.'

'Did your mother not say anything in her letters?'

'No.'

On the first day of the journey home, Karo tried not

to think too much about Hamburg. It was hard enough. But on the second day, she was so tense that she couldn't think of anything else. Would she live at home again? Or go back to Grandpa? Or would she really go to boarding school? She didn't even know what she wanted any more.

As they turned into Kuhnsweg, she closed her eyes for a moment. She hoped there wouldn't be another row straight off.

After she'd rung the doorbell, Mum came running straight down the stairs. She put her arms around Karo and gave her a hug.

'My Karo,' she murmured. 'I'm so glad you're back.'

She invited the Wiecherts to come up to the flat, but they wanted to go home.

'Bye,' said Rike, punching her lightly. 'I'll ring you tomorrow.'

'We'll miss you,' said Frau Wiechert.

'Yes,' said Herr Wiechert. 'And Max will too.'

Max licked her goodbye, right on the face. That made Karo laugh.

'Let me get a look at you,' said Mum on the way upstairs. 'I don't think you've ever had such a tan.'

'It was sunny the whole time.'

'Which is more than can be said for Boltenhagen.'

'Did you enjoy it anyway?'

'Yes.'

They'd almost reached their floor. Was Martin going

to put in an appearance immediately?

'Martin is in Berlin, by the way,' said Mum, as if she could read Karo's mind.

'Did he go away on purpose?'

'No, he has business to attend to in Berlin.'

That made it a bit easier.

'Welcome home.'

In Karo's room was a bunch of sweet peas, Karo's favourite flowers. And a Toblerone lay beside it.

Karo had brought Mum a jar of honey and a wooden honey spoon. She'd got them both in the market at Soulac. Mum loved honey more than anything.

'Thank you,' she said, with a beam.

At supper, Karo told Mum all about France and Mum told Karo all about Boltenhagen. Karo noticed that Mum hardly said a word about Martin; she only talked about Mecklenburg and the ocean and the guesthouse where they'd stayed. Had she fallen out with Martin?

'Maybe she didn't have such a great holiday at all,' said Karo to Rike the next day.

They were lying on the grass by the pool, freezing, because it wasn't anywhere nearly as warm in Hamburg as in Soulac.

'Would you like that?'

'I don't know.'

'If the two of them aren't getting along any more,

then everything would be the same as it was before.'

'No,' said Karo. 'It wouldn't.'

'Why not?'

'Now I know that he exists.'

'That's true.'

On the way home, Karo wondered if she should just ask Mum straight out. But that would be a bit weird after she'd wanted nothing to do with Martin for so long.

Nearly a week went by without Mum saying anything about Martin. And then one evening the phone rang. It must be Rike, thought Karo, running to the phone before Mum could get to it.

'Karo Delius.'

'Good evening, Karoline. It's Martin.'

'Eh ...'

'I ...'

'Mum's right here.'

'Just a moment,' said Martin.

Mum looked at her questioningly, but Karo shrugged her shoulders.

'I would like to ask you something.'

'What?'

'If you would mind my coming to visit you in Hamburg next weekend.'

Karo gulped.

'I'll only come if you agree to it.'

Did she agree to it? She didn't know.

'You don't have to answer now.'

'Well, then, I'll hand you over to Mum.'

She gave Mum the receiver and ran into her room.

Oddly, his voice hadn't sounded half as annoying as she had remembered.

Through the window, she could see old Herr Zeuner tottering after his fighting cats in his long-johns. He was waving his stick in the air.

Did she want Martin to come? Come to think of it, when had she last seen him? In the library? No, on the street, in Mühlenkamp, with Mum outside the flower shop, with his arms full of the potted Paris daisy.

Karo lay on her bed and stared at the ceiling. All the little cracks were still there. But they hadn't got any bigger. What should she do now? She had to say something.

'When will you be speaking to Martin again?' Karo asked when Mum came in to say good night.

'Tomorrow evening.'

'Then, tell him that, as far as I am concerned, he can come to Hamburg.'

'He will be pleased.'

'We don't have to do anything together, do we?'

Mum smiled. 'Of course not.'

Rike was delighted when Karo told her what had happened.

'Super! So when is he coming?'

'On Saturday, I think.'

'It'll be great, you'll see.'

'How do you know?'

'I just have a good feeling about it.'

'Now I'm really nervous.'

'I bet you your father is nice.'

'What makes you think that?'

'He just looked nice that time I saw him on the Alster.'

The days went by much more slowly than usual. Karo just wished the whole thing was over.

'Martin is arriving at the central station at a few minutes to two,' said Mum at breakfast on Saturday. 'I'm collecting him.'

Karo nodded and put the roll she'd already bitten into back on her plate. She had decided that morning, when she woke up, that she wasn't going to the station to meet Martin. It would be such a drag.

'Will you be home this afternoon?'

'Yes.'

'Well, then, we'll come straight here.'

'But I don't want to be having tea and cake with you two, or anything like that.'

'No.'

'You look as if that is exactly what you had planned.'

'Karo, the situation is difficult for me too.'

'You'd be better off not organising anything.'

'Fine.'

The nearer Martin's arrival got, the more nervous Karo became. She rode around the block on her bike, bought herself a chocolate ice-cream and rang Rike from a public phone.

'I'm a bundle of nerves.'

'When is he coming?'

'My mother is picking him up from the central station just before two.'

'But you don't want to go.'

'I don't want to do anything as a threesome.'

'Well, then, do something with him, just the two of you.'

'So what should I say to him?'

'I don't know ... but he is probably just as nervous as you are.'

'I suppose.'

'Maybe just wait and see.'

'Hm ...'

'Well, good luck. I'll be thinking of you.'

'Thanks,' said Karo and hung up. She felt a bit better.

When she got home, Mum was already long gone to the station. There was a note on the kitchen table to say that if she was hungry she could heat up some left-over carrot stew. If she was hungry! Apart from a quarter of a bread roll and the chocolate ice-cream, she'd eaten nothing today. She turned on the stove and got a plate out of the cupboard.

While she was eating, she kept wondering if she heard steps on the stairs. And if so, would they stop outside their flat? Ten to three. It couldn't go on much longer.

She cleared away her dishes into the dishwasher and ran out onto the balcony. From here, you could see the whole of Kuhnsweg. Karo's eyes roamed around, but there was no sign of Mum's navy blue Golf. If only they would come, so that at least the meeting and greeting would be over. Or had they gone off some place? Karo pulled a few withered flowers off the Paris daisy. No, if that was the case, Mum wouldn't have asked her if she'd be home in the afternoon.

At that moment, she saw the Golf coming into the Kuhnsweg. Until two minutes ago, there'd been a parking spot just opposite, but now there wasn't a place to be found. Mum drove slowly past the parked cars, turned right at the end of the street and reappeared two minutes later at the other end. Still no parking places. She'll be cursing, thought Karo. At least, she cursed when Karo was with her. Maybe it was different when she was with Martin? She didn't know. Suddenly the car stopped in the middle of the street, the passenger door opened and Martin got out. Why did he have to wear that terrible anorak? He opened the boot and took out a briefcase and a suitcase. Mum waved at him, wound up her window and drove on.

When Martin arrived at the front door, he stopped and looked up.

'Hallo, Karoline,' he called.

'Afternoon.'

'My train was late.'

'I see.'

He disappeared into the doorway. Karo ran out into the hall. She could hear his footsteps. He'd be on the second floor in a moment. Should she open the door for him or let him unlock it for himself?

She opened the door and held her breath for a couple of seconds. It wasn't going to be too bad.

He'd reached the top step, and he smiled when he saw her. 'Here I am,' he said, putting his luggage down.

Karo put out her hand to him, because she couldn't think of anything else to do. He took her hand in his two hands and pressed it.

'Aren't you going to come in?' asked Karo pointing at the luggage.

He nodded and took his things into Mum's room.

'Are you thirsty?'

'Yes.'

'We have Coke, milk, apple juice, orange juice, sparkling water and tea.'

'Sparkling water.'

He came into the kitchen with her and sat on the chair at the window. 'Are the cats still there?'

'Yes. They were fighting again a few days ago.' Karo gave him the glass and poured a glass of Coke for herself.

'We used to have a cat,' said Martin.

'And ... did she die?'

'No, she lives with my son. After the divorce, he took her with him when he went with his mother to live with his grandparents.'

'What's he called? Your son, I mean.'

'Andreas.'

'What age is he?'

'Seventeen.'

At that moment, the door was unlocked.

'Hello!' called Mum happily. 'Where are you?'

Karo wished she'd taken a bit longer to find a parking space.

Then they did have tea and cake after all, Karo's favourite: raspberry, blackberry and blackcurrant on a shortbread base. But Mum talked all the time, just as Karo knew she would. About late trains and the lack of parking spaces and old Herr Zeuner's fighting cats. And when she'd said all that, she started talking about Karo's holiday in France. At some point, Karo couldn't stand it any longer and went to her room.

At supper it was much the same. Karo longed to tell her to shut her mouth for a few minutes. All this chatter was surely driving Martin mad too.

'Should we go and get an ice-cream, do you think?' Mum suggested after a while.

Karo shook her head.

'Normally, you can't get enough ice-cream' said Mum in astonishment.

'I don't feel like it this evening,' muttered Karo.

When she went to bed that night, she thought about what Martin had told her before Mum came in. Maybe she'd try to get a chance to talk to him again.

THE FILM

The next morning, Karo and Rike met, with their bikes, at the Krugkoppel Bridge. It looked like rain, so Karo hadn't brought her swimming things.

'So, how did it go?' asked Rike.

'Fine. As long as my mother wasn't there – she was looking for a place to park. But as soon as she arrived into the flat, she just rabbited on and on. And Martin and I couldn't get a word in edgeways.'

'She must have been in a state, your mother.'

'Hm ...'

'How long is he staying?'

Karo shrugged. 'He brought a suitcase.'

'Well, then, he's not planning to leave soon.'

'Nah.'

'Will we go for a ride around the Alster?'

'OK.'

They pedalled off.

'What does your father do, anyway?' asked Rike after a while.

Karo had been wondering about that herself.

'It's kind of weird, the way he is able to hang around here.'

'Maybe he's unemployed.'

'Don't think so.'

'Why not?'

'Dunno.'

No. If Karo was honest, she didn't believe that either. Yesterday afternoon, she'd seen Martin leafing through some files or other. It looked as if some people could just take their work with them, wherever they happened to be.

That evening, Mum announced that she and Martin were going out. She was wearing a new green silk blouse, tight trousers and court shoes.

'You look very smart.'

'Thanks.'

'Where are you going?'

Mum hesitated. 'Eh ... to the pictures.'

Karo nearly asked if she could come too, but Mum looked as if she'd prefer to go with Martin on her own.

Karo had been asleep. She woke up, knowing that Mum was tiptoeing into her room.

'I just wanted to tuck you in.'

'Was the film good?'

Mum nodded and gave her a goodnight kiss. Karo could see that she had been crying.

'What's wrong?'

Mum stroked her hair. 'Nothing. Go back to sleep.'

Karo turned onto her side and closed her eyes. It was only then that it occurred to her: she'd forgotten to ask her what kind of a movie it had been.

When Karo saw the green blouse hanging in Mum's room the next day, she remembered how she'd thought Mum had been crying the previous evening. Was the film so sad, or had Mum and Martin been quarrelling?

At that moment, she heard the two of them laughing together in the kitchen.

Relieved, Karo went back to her room. Whatever had happened yesterday evening, the main thing was everything was fine again.

She looked down into the courtyard. The cats were, for once, lying peacefully together in the sunshine. Every time she caught sight of the cats now, they reminded her of Martin, who had lost his cat, together with his son. When would she manage to have a word with him again in private?

A few days later, Karo saw Martin reading the paper in the kitchen. Mum had gone to see a colleague. They were planning a new course together.

'I ... wanted to ask you something,' said Karo, sitting down beside Martin at the table.

'Ask away,' he said, putting his paper down.

'What do you do for a living?'

'I'm a director.'

Karo stared at him, her mouth open. 'A director?'

'Yes. I make films.'

'What kind of films?'

'Feature films. For the cinema.'

'And ... how do you do that? ... How do you make a movie?'

'It's a long process. First, you need a good script. Either you write it yourself, or you get it from a scriptwriter. Then you have to decide which scenes have to be made on location and which in studio. And then you have to start looking for suitable locations and actors. The main thing you need is someone to pay the expenses. So far, I've been lucky, because I was employed by DEFA in Babelsberg. But I don't know how that is going to work out in the future.'

'Where is Babelsberg?'

'In Potsdam.'

Karo suddenly saw Martin as she had seen him in the library, looking at her in amazement. Maybe he hadn't been spying on her after all. Maybe he really had been working.

'Do you write your own scripts?'

'Yes ... because I want to film my own stories.'

'And are you making a film at the moment?'

'No. At the moment, I'm writing a new script. Unfortunately, I've got all tangled up in the story.'

'What kind of a story is it?'

'It's set in Berlin and it's about a little boy who loses his father in February 1946. He dies of typhus. His mother is also very weak, and, to avoid starving, the boy gets involved in trading on the black market.'

'What is he trading in?'

'Whatever his family still has. Silverware, rugs, jewellery. Sometimes someone gives him a few cigarettes. They're easily traded for food.' Martin stroked his bald head with his hand. 'And he nicks coal for the stove, as do lots of other people. There was an unbelievably cold winter in 1945/46.'

'So my grandpa has told me.'

'Yes. Your grandpa and I often talk about these things. He remembers it all very clearly.'

'And why have you got so caught up in this story?'

'The longer I work on the script, the more I am moved by the theme. That's why it's all going so slowly.'

'How did you come across this story?'

'I traded on the black market myself when I was a child.'

'And did you ... did you also lose your father?'

'No. Fortunately not. But a friend of mine did.'

'How old was he?'

'Six. Same age as myself.'

Karo started counting. If he was six at that time, then he must be fifty now.

Martin smiled. 'As far as you are concerned, I'm ancient. Right?'

'Oh, not too ancient. Rike's father is fifty-two.'

'That reminds me ... Would you like to have Rike around some time? I'd like to get to know her.'

'Yes. She'd like to meet you too.'

Karo tried a few times to ring Rike to invite her, but the Wiecherts were never at home.

So what should she do now? She really wanted to talk to someone about what Martin had said to her.

Maybe she should go to see Grandpa. She hadn't seen him for ages. Not since before the holidays, when she'd been living with him.

'Do you like honey custard cake?' asked Grandpa when she arrived.

'Mmmm, delicious!'

'Well, serve yourself!'

Karo didn't need to be told twice.

'Will you have juice or cocoa?'

'Juice.'

While Grandpa was making tea for himself, Karo mixed her favourite drink – apple juice with sparkling water.

'And ... how are things at home?'

'Not too bad.'

'Your mum is so happy that you are back living with her.'

'Hm.'

'Though of course it was lovely here, just the two of us.'

Karo swallowed hard. 'Grandpa?'

'Yes?'

'Have you known all along that Martin makes films?'

'Yes. We often talk about his new script.'

'I only found out today.'

'Ach! So then you weren't there?'

'Where?'

'At the cinema.'

'When?'

'Last Sunday, I think.'

Karo shook her head. Last Sunday? That was the evening that Mum had looked as if she'd been crying.

'A film was shown here in Hamburg. One Martin made years ago.'

'Is it still running?'

'I couldn't say.'

On her way home, Karo picked up a cinema programme. In the Holi, in the Grindel and in the Abaton there were no films by Martin. Those were the cinemas that Karo knew best. Suddenly she jumped.

The Metropolis was showing a film in the afternoon. A film called *Lost*. Director: M. Klessmann, 1981.

She had to ring Rike immediately and ask her if she would go to the cinema with her the next day. Luckily, she was at home.

'What kind of a film is it?'

'It's called *Lost*.'

'Never heard of it.'

'Me neither. Please come. It's important.'

'All right.'

'Meet you at half past three on Krugkoppel Bridge?'

'Right. See you then.'

It took Karo ages to get to sleep that night. Suppose it was a very sad film? After all, Mum had cried so much that her eyes had been all red when she came home.

'Where's Martin?' asked Karo, when she came into the kitchen the next morning.

'He's left.'

'Where did he go?'

'To the city archive. He needs to look something up, because he'll be gone by Sunday evening.'

'Oh, I didn't know.'

'He has some important meetings in Berlin next week.'

Pity, thought Karo. Just as she was getting used to Martin.

'What are you planning to do today?' asked Mum.

'I'm meeting Rike at half three.'

'Going swimming?'

Karo hesitated. 'We'll see.'

She was the first at the Krugkoppel Bridge. She hoped Rike wouldn't be too late. It took at least a quarter of an hour to get to the Metropolis.

It was twenty to four when Rike finally arrived, totally out of breath.

'Sorry. Max ran away. We had to look for him.'

'And? Did you find him?'

'Yes. The kids next door had lured him into their house with a sausage.'

Karo got up on her bike. 'Come on, we have to hurry.'

'What kind of a film is it?'

'It's by my father.'

'Whaaat? Your father makes movies?'

'Yeah. I only found out yesterday.'

'Well, let's get a move on!'

It was two minutes to four when they arrived at the Metropolis. They bought their tickets and went into an almost empty auditorium. So few people, Karo thought. Funny, that. Until very recently, she'd have been delighted to hear that a film of Martin's played to an audience of exactly seven.

'Any idea what it's about?'

'No. It just said something about a love story in the brochure – with a German–German background.'

'Did your father not say anything else about it?'

'I didn't tell him that I was going to see one of his films. Or my mother either.'

'Are you excited?'

'Mmm ...'

It got dark in the auditorium and the first trailer appeared on the screen. Karo suddenly came out in a sweat. 1981 ... German–German background? How come she'd never thought of it before?

'What's wrong?' asked Rike.

'I'm ... dizzy.'

'Do you want to go?'

'No.'

Karo stared at the screen. Now it said DEFA-Deutsche Film AG in glowing white letters.

Lost – Written and directed by Martin Klessmann.

Black-and-white pictures of a snow-covered city. A river, a bridge, in the background a big old building. A couple is standing hand in hand on the riverbank, looking at the water. She's young, much younger than he is. Her long hair is fluttering in the wind. She's wearing a woollen scarf around her neck, a striped scarf ...

Karo held her breath. Mum used to have a scarf like that. There was a photo of the two of them, when she was still very small. They're standing on the frozen Alster, Karo is waving at the camera and Mum is wrapping the scarf around her head.

As if in a dream, Karo watched the images drifting

past her, images of a lake, an allotment, a cemetery. And all the time, the couple, laughing and kissing and embracing as if they would never let each other go.

Everyone else seemed to be far, far away. There was, at the most, a waiter, a porter or a man in the allotment, with whom they exchanged a few words. Otherwise, they sat on a sofa in the allotment hut, went walking in the cemetery, talked, read and kissed.

Karo noticed that she was starting to get impatient. It wasn't a normal life they were living. What did they do in between sitting around together on a sofa? Where did they live, where did they work, where did they meet their friends?

And then the Wall suddenly appeared. No more sound ... nothing ... only the Wall, dividing the screen into two parts.

Karo could feel her pulse beating in her temples. She had to force herself not to close her eyes, even though her head hurt.

Now came lots of scenes showing the man and the woman separated. The woman in the library, at her desk, with a friend. The man with a movie camera, with his little boy, with his wife.

When the couple met again, they rowed. They both talked, they both screamed, neither listened to the other. And then the Wall again.

The last image showed a man standing at a border-crossing, watching visitors from the West meeting their friends and relations. The man seemed to be waiting for someone, but no one came.

Tears were running down Karo's cheeks. She had no idea what was written on the screen at the end.

'Did you see what it said there?' asked Rike, as they came out.

Karo shook her head.

'The film was banned immediately in 1981 and only had its premiere in February 1990.' She turned to Karo. 'Hey, Karo, you're crying.'

Now Karo's tears really started to flow. Rike put her arms around her and stroked her back. They stood like that until Karo finally stopped crying.

'I ... I had no idea that ... it would be ... like that,' she said, trying to smile.

'Will we go and get something to drink?'
'OK.'

There was an ice-cream parlour not far away. They found a seat at the very back and ordered two Cokes.

'A mad story, really,' said Rike.

Karo nodded.

'Do you think it was really like that?'
'I don't know.'
'Then you'd have a half-brother.'
'So I have.'
'Really?'
'Yes.'
'What age is he?'

'Seventeen.'

'Have you ever met him?'

'Nah. He lives in Berlin, with his mother and his grandparents.'

'Not with your dad?'

Karo shook her head. 'My father and that woman have been divorced for ages.'

'Because of your mother?'

'Hm.' Karo drank up her Coke in one go. 'Martin asked me yesterday if you'd like to come around some time.'

'For sure.'

'Maybe the next time he's in Hamburg.'

'How do you mean? Is he going away again?'

'Yes, on Sunday.'

'Tell him to come back soon.'

'I will,' said Karo, wiping her tears away.

'Did you go swimming?' asked Mum when Karo got home.

'Nah ...'

'Well, then, where were you?'

'We went cycling,' muttered Karo, and she went into her room.

She couldn't tell Mum that they'd been to see Martin's film. That would make her cry again, and she didn't want to do that. Mum didn't have to know how sad she'd found the story.

PICNIC ON THE ELBE

It was sunny that weekend and really warm again.

'Will we go out to the Elbe?' asked Karo at breakfast.

'I promised Grandpa that I'd do a big shop with him today,' said Mum.

'Karo and I could go on our own,' Martin suggested.

'Yes,' said Karo. 'We could have a picnic.'

'You should take the train,' said Mum.

Karo shook her head. 'It's nicer on the bus.'

'I think so too,' said Martin.

'It'll take for ever on the bus.'

'Doesn't matter,' said Karo, looking up the bus timetable.

'What do you want in your sandwiches?' asked Martin.

'Ham and camembert.'

'And what kind of fruit?'

'Apples.'

Karo put in a bottle of water too and a bar of nut chocolate.

They took the 106 as far as Eppendorfer Market and from there they changed to the 39 to Teufelsbrück. At first, Karo wondered what would happen if someone from school got onto the bus. But then after a little while she started to think about other things.

'Where did you first meet Mum?'

'In a bookshop on Alexanderplatz. It was an icy cold day in February 1978.'

'And what was she doing in East Berlin? She was at university in West Berlin.'

'Yes, but she'd got a one-day visa for East Berlin. She'd never been on the other side of the city.'

'Did you speak to her?'

'Yes,' said Martin with a grin. 'She looked so lost, standing there in front of those bookshelves full of Marx and Engels. I asked her if she was looking for something in particular. Yes, she said, pointing to a sign hanging over the bookshelves that said Classics. In the West, classics are books by Goethe and Schiller. I explained that we meant something different and that each Germany had its own classics. That made us both laugh, and then we went and had a cup of coffee.'

'Did you fall in love with her that day?'

'Yes.'

'And when did she come back?'

'A week later. And after that, she came every week.'

Should she ask him about the scarf and the sofa and the walks in the cemetery?

Just then, the bus stopped at Teufelsbrück.

'Are we there already?' asked Martin.

Karo nodded. The journey had seemed much shorter than usual.

They walked along the Elbe to the little beach with the weeping willow that Karo loved so much.

'Will we sit here in the shade?'

Martin nodded. They unpacked their sandwiches and began to eat.

'Was there really an allotment?' asked Karo after a while.

Martin looked astonished 'Did ... Jutta tell you about that?'

'No.'

'But then how do you know?'

'I just do.'

'Were you at the pictures lately, by any chance?'

'Could have been.'

'You know, Jutta and I wondered if we shouldn't all go to see the film together.'

'I wouldn't have liked that.'

'No. She didn't want to either.'

'So tell me, what was it like?'

'The allotments are called Grönland. A colleague of mine had a hut there, in which we could meet.'

'Is that where I was conceived?'

'Yes.'

'And this Grönland, is it still there?'

'Yes. Jutta and I were there in the summer.'

'I'd like to go there some day.'

'Well, suppose you both came to Berlin for a weekend?'

'Yeah.' Karo took an apple. 'Why were you nearly the whole time in that hut, by the way?'

'I was afraid of the state security. There were often problems with that crowd. One of my films had just been banned.'

'And this one too?'

'Yes, this one was really and truly banned. It was classified as anti-state. And so it was. I never had a very good relationship with the state.'

'Did you ever think of escaping?'

'Yes, but I didn't have the courage. And in any case, the outlook wasn't good. My letters to Jutta all came back. I couldn't assume that she still loved me.'

'So, when did you start to look for her?'

'The night the Wall came down. I knew that Jutta came from Hamburg. So the very next day I went to West Berlin and looked up her address in the Hamburg phonebook. After that, I tried a few times to write letters, but it didn't work, so then late one evening I just rang up.'

'And?'

'And nothing. I hung up before anyone could answer.'

'Why?'

'Because I was afraid.'

'So what were you thinking?'

'Ach, all kinds of things. That Jutta had a partner, or even that she'd been happily married for years with lots of children. But I never thought that we could have a child.'

'Weird.'

'I still think it's weird.'

'So when did you decide to come to Hamburg?'

'On the second of May, very early in the morning. And then I just went. Of course, I didn't know if I would be able to do it – to ring your doorbell. I'd stood outside your house for a few hours at the end of March.'

'Really?'

'Yes.'

'And ... did you see Mum?'

'No.'

'If I'd known all along that you were alive, I might have come to see you.'

Martin looked at her and nodded. 'Jutta really blames herself that she allowed you to grow up with this fib about a dead father.'

'Still?'

'Yes. She thinks that was the main reason why you found it so difficult to get used to me.'

'Hm ...'

'She tried to wipe me out of her life because that was the only way she could cope with the separation. I don't know if you can understand that.'

'Yes ... but hadn't she been afraid that you would turn up one day?'

'Karoline, nobody had the slightest notion that that border would ever be opened.'

'Did you miss Mum terribly?'

'Yes. The separation nearly did my head in.'

'Why did you make that film?'

'To free myself of the whole business.'

'And did it work?'

'No.'

Karo lay down on the sand and looked up into the tree. 'What was going on with that row at the end of the film?'

'It was terrible,' said Martin, his voice breaking. 'I had told Jutta that I was going to Leningrad in the summer to make a film, and she came up with the idea that she would visit me there, and we would finally have some proper time together. I told her that wouldn't work, because I had already organised for my family to come with me to Leningrad. Jutta took that as proof that I wasn't loyal to her, that my family was more important to me. It wasn't true. I was just too spineless to tell my wife that I loved someone else. I only told her that after Jutta had gone. We got divorced a year later.'

'Does your son know about me and Mum?'

'I just told him recently.'

'And?'

'Well, he wasn't exactly thrilled to find out that I have a second child. But he wasn't much surprised either. Maybe he'd already guessed something like that, unlike myself.'

'And ... are you on good terms now?'

'Not too bad. I've seen far too little of Andreas in the last eleven years.'

'Do you think I can meet him sometime?'

'Yes, sometime. But for the moment he needs a bit of time to digest the whole thing.'

'I can understand that.'

Martin grinned. 'Yes, you're the expert at that.'

'Will we walk on a bit?'

'Yes.'

They stood up, packed up the remains of their picnic and went on.

In the shade, Karo hadn't noticed how hot it had got. The air shimmered with heat. In the distance sailed a cargo ship, getting smaller and smaller. Karo suddenly remembered that Martin was going back to Berlin the following evening.

'Will you come back next weekend?'

'I think so.'

'G

HAMBURG OR BERLIN?

Chaos reigned in Karo's room on Sunday evening. As always at the end of the holidays, it took for ever for her to get all her things for school together.

She opened the drawer of her desk, looking for her set square, and got a shock. The chain! It was lying there where she had thrown it after Martin had first appeared.

She fingered the aquamarine gently. What would Martin say if she wore the chain? After all, he'd given it to Mum, not to her.

Karo put it around her neck and looked in the mirror. Maybe he wouldn't even remember it.

'Hey, I recognise that chain,' said Martin, when they picked him up from the station on Friday evening.

'Mum gave it to me for my last birthday.'

'Did you know that it had come from me?'

Karo nodded.

'You were so thrilled,' said Mum.

'Yes, because I finally had something from my father.'

'The dead father.'

'Ye-es.'

'And when he suddenly came alive, the first thing you did was to take off the chain.'

'Exactly.'

Martin laughed. 'Well, try to explain that!'

'I'd rather not.'

'In any case, it suits you very well.'

'Thank you.'

Karo had thought they might hire a rowing boat when Rike came round on Saturday. But on that very day, it started to rain heavily.

'We'll just have to stay indoors,' said Mum. 'Is that a problem?'

'No, but I don't want to just sit around jabbering.'

When the doorbell rang, Karo was so nervous her hands were damp. That had never happened before just because she was going to see Rike. If only it wouldn't be a boring old afternoon! It was never boring at the Wiecherts'.

But as it turned out, everything went smoothly. While Karo was getting the plum cake from the kitchen, she heard Martin and Rike laughing about something. And later, when they were playing rummy, they all laughed a lot.

'It was fun, wasn't it?' asked Mum when she went to say good night to Karo in bed.

'Yes.'

'Martin and I were just thinking of something.'

'What?'

'That we could go to Berlin next weekend.'

'Fab!'

'If you like, Rike could come too.'

'Really?'

'Yes. Martin's flat is big enough for us all.'

'I'll ask her tomorrow.'

Luckily the next morning was sunny. Karo could hardly wait to see Rike at the pool.

'Are you off already?' asked Mum. 'It's only half past.'

'It doesn't matter,' said Karo running down to the basement.

When she came back up with her bike, Frau Becker was in the entrance hall, stroking that dog of hers.

'It looks as if the lover has turned into something a bit more permanent,' she said with a smirk.

'That's not her lover. That's my father,' said Karo.

'Your father?' cried Frau Becker in amazement. 'I thought he was dead.'

'We all make mistakes,' said Karo and pushed her bicycle past the astonished Frau Becker.

Rike was waiting just at the entrance to the swimming pool.

'You're wearing your chain again,' she said by way of greeting. 'Looks good.'

'Thanks.'

'Your father is really nice.'

'He and my mother have had an idea.'

'What?'

'We're all going to Berlin together.'

'Me too?'

'Yes, next weekend.'

'Hey, that'd be fantastic!'

'Do you think your parents will let you?'

'For sure. I'll ring them now, just to check.'

When Rike came back from making the phone call, she was beaming. 'No problem.'

'Hurray!' cried Karo jumping up and down. 'Come on, into the water!'

The day flew by. At lunchtime, Karo and Rike had chips with ketchup. And in the afternoon, they were dying for an ice-cream.

On the way home, they went together as far as Krugkoppel Bridge. They leant their bicycles on the bridge wall and looked into the water, which reflected the sunlight.

'Do you know how it's all going to work out with you guys?' asked Rike.

'How do you mean?'

'I was just thinking ... because your father lives in Berlin and you are in Hamburg ...'

'So what?'

'Would you not be afraid that you'll move to Berlin some day?'

Karo's ears started to buzz. She'd never even thought of such a thing!

'What'd we do then?' asked Rike.

'I don't know,' said Karo

'Have your parents said anything about that?'

Karo shook her head. But Mum had said yesterday that Martin had a big flat.

'But maybe you'll stay here.'

Karo nodded, but her good mood had evaporated.

'You're not eating,' said Mum at supper. 'Is something wrong?'

Karo took a deep breath. 'I was talking to Rike today ...'

'Is she not able to come to Berlin?' asked Martin.

'No, she can.'

'But ...'

'She was wondering if we might be moving to Berlin sometime.'

Mum and Martin looked at each other. Had they already planned this?

'We haven't made any decisions,' said Mum. 'What have you been thinking?'

'I don't want to leave Hamburg.'

'No, me neither. And anyway it would be very difficult with my job.'

Karo breathed out.

'And I want to hang onto my flat in Berlin,' said Martin. 'For the moment, it looks as if I will go on making my films there. At the same time, I would of course like to spend more time in Hamburg.'

'Have we enough money for a bigger place?' asked Karo.

Mum shook her head.

'Well, then, Martin will just have to move into our living room. And we can go to Berlin every now and again.'

Martin smiled. 'You wouldn't have said that a few weeks back.'

'Nah. Definitely not.'

'I wouldn't have dared to suggest it even today,' said Mum.

Karo grinned. 'I raised merry hell, didn't I?'

'Yes!' cried Mum.

'You made things pretty bad for me too,' Karo added.

Martin nodded. 'Sometimes, I thought I should never have come.'

It was very quiet for a moment. Karo could feel her heart beating. 'But it's good that you did,' she said, taking a piece of bread. Because suddenly she felt hungry.